At Summer's End

Rachael O. Phillips

Annie's®
AnniesFiction.com

Books in The Inn at Magnolia Harbor series

Where Hope Blooms
Safe Harbor
Binding Vows
Tender Melody
At Summer's End
Mending the Past
Kindred Blessings

. . . and more to come!

Library of Congress-in-Publication Data
At Summer's End / by Rachael O. Phillips
p. cm.
I. Title
2019942491

AnniesFiction.com
(800) 282-6643
The Inn at Magnolia Harbor™
Series Creator: Shari Lohner
Editor: Lorie Jones
Cover Illustrator: Bonnie Leick

10 11 12 13 14 | Printed in China | 9 8 7 6 5 4 3 2 1

Grace

"When you buy a gorgeous chandelier, nobody ever tells you that you'll have to dust it." Grace Porter grasped the ladder's top rung, knuckles whitening, and extended her long-handled duster toward the sparkling antique prisms that adorned the foyer in the Magnolia Harbor Inn.

"You did draw the tough job," her younger sister, Charlotte Wylde, admitted as she dusted the stairway's ornate black-iron bannister. "You'll just have to get better at rock-paper-scissors."

"That game never did make sense to me." If Grace had dared, she would have shot Charlotte an excellent imitation of their late mother's gentle yet potent glance. But given her position ten feet above the polished, white marble floor, Grace kept her gaze fixed on the chandelier as she methodically wiped every single crystal. How many were there? Two hundred? Three hundred?

Charlotte scrubbed the bannister's vine-like sections with an old toothbrush, occasionally pausing to stretch her slender frame. "Thank goodness for air-conditioning in August. And thank goodness there's more to owning an inn than dusting."

"But we're so good at it," Grace kidded as she shifted position. She aimed a smile at her sister. "You're even better at cooking."

Charlotte, who had written three best-selling cookbooks, loved whipping up unique breakfasts for their guests. Grace had given up figuring out how Charlotte, who baked with who-cares-about-calories abandon, stayed so thin.

"We'd have gone nowhere in this business if you didn't work your people magic," Charlotte said. "I don't think you or Winston have ever met a grouchy guest you couldn't charm within two minutes."

Hearing his name, Winston gave a staccato bark and entered, his little claws clicking against the shiny floor. The shih tzu mix glanced from human to human with a supervisory air. At the sight of Grace on the ladder, Winston cocked his head, as if to ask how she'd grown long metal legs. He bounded up the staircase to Charlotte.

"I thought you were taking a nap in the living room." Charlotte scratched behind his fluffy ears, then turned to Grace. "I swear this dog knows what we're going to say before we do."

"He's smart all right." Having finally finished the chandelier, Grace carefully backed down the ladder. "Is he wasting the morning dusting? No. He's been snoozing."

Winston dashed down the stairs and nosed Grace's hand before returning to the living room.

Grinning, Grace consulted the to-do list on her smartphone. "Okay, we've finished the foyer, except for the last-minute sweeping and touch-up."

"It actually sounds pretty easy after painting all those railings on the porches." Descending the stairs, Charlotte groaned as she shrugged stiffness from her shoulders. "Two stories' worth. I'll never get used to it."

"True. But we saved a bundle by doing it ourselves," Grace reminded her. "Maybe this fall, we can line up Tammy and her crew to shampoo the carpets." Tammy Snyder owned Helping Hands Cleaning, a local maid service they occasionally hired.

"Really? You mean we don't have to do everything ourselves?" Charlotte gave Grace a teasing poke.

Grace poked back. Some sister things never changed, which was one reason why she so enjoyed running the inn with Charlotte.

"While I was wielding the toothbrush up there, I thought about the enjoyable part of what we do." Charlotte gazed dreamily through the French doors that comprised the antebellum mansion's entrance.

Grace smiled. "Like the Candlelight Journey Festival. I can't wait."

Magnolia Harbor's August celebration featured a deliciously spooky walk that took participants back to the era of the Revolutionary War. Tourists flooded the small South Carolina town, and their bed-and-breakfast was always booked. Guests enjoyed perusing the charming shops and booths in the historic downtown. They also took full advantage of Lake Haven. Its blue-green waters lapped along the inn's backyard and private dock.

It was a busy time for innkeepers, but Grace and Charlotte were usually able to slip away for a little while to sample the exciting side of the festival.

"I've thought up the most marvelous recipe for blini with caviar for our party," Charlotte said.

Caviar. Grace tried to suppress her sigh. Though her sister exhibited great money sense most of the time, Charlotte's common sense sometimes evaporated when it came to pricey foods—especially when she wanted to throw a big party. Grace knew that Charlotte planned to pull out all the stops during the Candlelight Journey Festival.

"I'll use sturgeon caviar," Charlotte continued, avoiding eye contact with Grace. "Not salmon. Otherwise, the taste isn't nearly as rich."

Grace's whole being longed for an icy glass of sweet tea without the controversy that sooner—not later—they'd have to settle. She picked her words like the best flowers from their gardens. "Everyone who tastes your creations will think they've gone to heaven." Grace gestured toward the kitchen. "Why don't I pour us a couple of glasses of tea? We'll sit and figure out exactly who the lucky people will be."

Charlotte narrowed her dark-brown eyes ever so slightly, but she followed Grace into the kitchen. The updated yet period atmosphere provided the ideal place for a friendly sister chat. Charlotte plopped onto an upholstered stool at the island while Grace brought over big mason jars full of tea and cracked ice.

Charlotte took a long sip. Then she gave Grace a smug smile. Apparently, she thought her menu of sturgeon caviar was already a done deal.

Grace gulped a huge swallow, hoping the tea's cool sweetness would saturate her voice—and temper. "Your hors d'oeuvres idea sounds wonderful, but I'm not sure how caviar fits into the historical context."

Though their mansion had been built in 1816, Grace and Charlotte had agreed to lean toward the Revolutionary War era during the Candlelight Journey Festival.

"It does fit," Charlotte retorted. "I do my research, thank you very much. Caviar was a favorite long before colonial times, and George Washington fished for sturgeon in the Potomac River."

"You're the expert," Grace said soothingly. "If we're going to do haute cuisine, we should probably keep the party a soiree—you know, intimate. Elegant." She flashed a smile that was gentle, loving, and with a touch of sanity Grace hoped would penetrate her sister's fantasies and deflate them to an appropriate size.

"How intimate are we talking?"

"Oh, I don't know." Grace shrugged. "A dozen people, give or take."

"Are you kidding?" Charlotte demanded. "Only a dozen—and that includes the guests staying here that weekend?"

"Well, maybe we can increase the guest list to twenty," Grace suggested. "It would make a diverse group, yet it would keep the party personal. Plus, it wouldn't break the bank."

"That makes no sense." Charlotte thumped her tea jar on the counter. "The whole purpose of this party is to increase our exposure."

"It is?" The words popped out before Grace could stop them.

"We need to be proactive in promoting our business," Charlotte stated. "Tourists jam this town during the festival. Families come home to Magnolia Harbor from Charleston and Atlanta and even Washington and New York."

"I know, but—"

"We want them to realize that this inn is the best place for their special occasions and business retreats," Charlotte interrupted. "It won't happen if we don't wow at least a hundred of them with a killer open house."

"A hundred?" Grace repeated.

Charlotte put her hands on her hips. "Do you want to make money or not?"

Though she was beginning to steam, Grace managed to keep her tone calm. "I suppose we do have to keep up with the competition. Like The Tidewater."

Grace referred to the small inn and restaurant on the other side of Lake Haven. Dean Bradley, the owner and chef, had once worked with Charlotte at Le Crabe Fou in Charleston, South Carolina. During their time at the upscale restaurant, there had been some bumps in their professional relationship. But now they helped each other out when needed and had a friendly rivalry over their cooking.

"You think I want to throw this party just because Dean's giving one?" Charlotte asked.

"You tell me."

"Dean's cooking can't begin to compete with mine," Charlotte said. "Yes, he trained at Le Cordon Bleu, but he's always overestimated his own abilities."

"I'll agree on both counts." Grace thought that Dean was pleasant and a great guy, but sometimes he seemed to suffer from an inflated ego.

"Plus, Dean's never worked as hard as I do to create original recipes." Charlotte pushed back a lock of blonde hair straying from her ponytail. "Instead of setting trends, he lets the trends rule him."

Grace sipped her tea and listened. She could have recited every word of this speech—she'd heard it repeatedly since Dean had worked under Charlotte at Le Crabe Fou—but she let her sister rant. Maybe if Charlotte transferred her ire to Dean, she'd feel less resentment toward Grace and her concerns.

She didn't believe it. But for a few more minutes, she could avoid the issue.

A renewed glare from Charlotte confirmed Grace's assessment. "Don't think I'll give in to your penny-pinching notions because I'm younger than you. If we want to attract the clientele we need, we have to take a few risks."

"And if we want to continue to thrive, we should stick to our budget," Grace said. "The budget we both agreed on."

"A *working* budget," Charlotte clarified. "Guidelines, not some bed-and-breakfast Ten Commandments that are chiseled in stone."

Someone knocked on the back door. "Hello?" called a familiar voice.

Winnie Bennett. With her smiles and humor, their aunt would soon have them both grinning. At least Grace hoped so. "I guess we can discuss this later," she said, setting her tea down on the counter.

"Discuss?" Charlotte echoed. "I'm not changing my mind."

Grace walked to the back door and opened it.

Her diminutive aunt stood there, holding an enormous tote. She smiled. "Good morning."

"Morning," Grace said as she relieved Winnie of the tote. "Did you carry this all the way here in the heat?" Winnie lived less than a mile away, but tote or no tote, nobody should walk that far this close to noon.

"Goodness, no. I drove." Winnie gave Grace a hug. "I brought your dresses over for the first fitting." Winnie, a master seamstress, had insisted on sewing their 1770s outfits for the festival.

"I can't wait to see them," Grace said. "Come in. Let me pour you a glass of tea." She led the way to the kitchen.

Grace took a glass pitcher of unsweetened tea from the refrigerator and poured its amber liquid into another icy mason jar for her aunt, who was greeting Charlotte.

"Thanks. Wish I could drink real tea," Winnie said, wiping her damp, beaming face, "but you know I have to keep a close watch on my sugar." She had diabetes, but she controlled it with diet and exercise. It meant she had to avoid the Southern tradition of sweet tea.

"It's more important that you stay healthy," Grace said as she picked up her own glass.

Winnie peered over her glass, searching Charlotte's face, then Grace's. "What's going on here? Are you fussing at each another?"

"Of course not," Grace replied. "Charlotte and I were just brainstorming some possibilities for the Candlelight Journey Festival."

"We're going to give the biggest and best party Magnolia Harbor's seen in decades," Charlotte declared.

Winnie arched her eyebrows as she dug into her tote. "Any guests around?"

"Not yet," Grace answered.

Winnie removed an unfinished spring-green taffeta gown and sage brocade petticoat. She held them up to Charlotte. "No sleeves yet. But I wanted to make sure I was headed in the right direction."

The elegant fabrics transferred their gentle glow to Charlotte's flinty dark eyes. Her golden hair shimmered against the dress's loveliness.

"Oh, Charlotte," Grace murmured. "It's perfect for you."

Her sister's tight mouth loosened into a smile.

Grace smothered a chuckle. Charlotte might try to cling to her anger, but how could she stay in a bad mood at the sight of a gorgeous new dress?

"Here's yours, Grace." Winnie extracted from her tote another vision in progress, a blue silk gown and silvery brocade petticoat. She glanced from the dress to Grace, and her voice softened. "I thought so. It's the exact shade of your eyes."

"It's beautiful," Grace gushed.

Winnie gazed at her nieces and smiled. "Your mother and I used to love to model dresses for each other when we were young."

Bittersweet scenes from her own childhood tugged at Grace. The three women stood silently for a moment thinking about Hazel Wylde—Winnie's sister and Grace and Charlotte's mother—who had passed away years before but was never far from their hearts.

"Well, are you two going to stand here all day before you try those on?" Winnie asked. She pulled out her tape measure and waved it threateningly.

Giggling like schoolgirls, Grace and Charlotte adjourned to Grace's private living quarters, donned Winnie's creations, and took turns letting Winnie tuck and pin.

Grace bent, shrugged, sat, stood, and turned at Winnie's command. How could her aunt possibly improve on the fit? The blue fabric hugged her frame without stretching or pulling, and the petticoat added exactly the right fullness.

Winnie showed her the dainty white lace she intended to use to edge the elbow-length sleeves, and Grace knew it would enhance the beautiful dress.

Charlotte's patience, however, was clearly beginning to ebb. Her smile faded, and Grace noted the return of less-than-friendly glances her way.

You think I've forgotten about the party? Charlotte's potent looks clearly communicated. *Well, think again.*

Winnie's delight in her gifts to them seemed to obstruct the initial X-ray vision that had detected their disagreement. Though Grace loved her aunt's visits, she employed her best hostess skills to move the fitting along without seeming to hurry Winnie. Soon her aunt walked out, smiling and hauling her tote.

Charlotte joined Grace on the porch. They waved to Winnie as she got into her car and drove away.

The minute Winnie's Toyota Camry disappeared, Charlotte turned to Grace. "I'm going home for a while." She lived in a small restored 1835 cottage on the inn's property. "You can text me later with what still needs to be done."

In other words, *I'll do my part, dear sister, but not alongside you.*

Grace nodded. "I could use a little break too."

Without another word, Charlotte marched toward her house.

Grace exhaled through gritted teeth as she watched her sister leave. A quick lunch and a good paddle in her kayak would probably stave off the small headache cyclones rotating in her temples.

But what would disperse this storm between her and Charlotte?

2

Grace

For the third time, Grace tweaked the sheer garlands she had draped from the tall posts of the Dogwood Suite's king-size bed. Now the tulle hung a little looser, with more graceful folds.

She stood back and studied the effect. It looked more like the results she'd envisioned. With the bed's antique coverlet and lace-edged linens, vintage photographs of brides and grooms, and luxuriant bouquets of lilies, asters, and zinnias she would arrange right before the honeymooners' arrival, the gold-and-white room would take on a decidedly romantic air.

For a moment, Grace simply stood still and admired its blend of elegance and welcome, hoping the young couple's stay would help start their life together on a positive note.

Memories of her own honeymoon decades earlier always stirred when she prepared rooms for newlyweds. If only she and Hank could have enjoyed more years together before his untimely death in a train accident.

But her life was good. Hank had given her their son, Jake, now a software programmer in Raleigh, North Carolina. And Grace was living out her dream of providing a haven where guests could relax and refresh.

She checked the palatial bathroom once more, inhaling the scent of candles and handmade soaps she'd arranged around its spa tub. The big basket of fluffy towels made her long for an hour of soaking in a soothing, fragrant bath.

But she didn't have time. Tom and Bonnie Klein were due at any moment. Had Charlotte finished the last-minute details in their suites?

Grace went to check. Her survey confirmed that Charlotte had covered her cleaning bases as always.

The Bluebell Suite—with its lake-colored walls, comfortable furniture, claw-foot bathtub, and tiled fireplace—was perfect from the gleaming hardwood floor to the dusted crystal chandelier. The elegant bath it shared with the Rosebud Suite, which included another claw-foot tub and a shower, appeared spotless. Though the Rosebud Suite wasn't as spacious as the Bluebell, Grace had always loved its rose-sprigged wallpaper, scalloped white coverlet, and embroidered floral linens and pillows.

The tall, shining windows reflected her furrowed forehead. Smoothing away unwelcome wrinkles, she suppressed a sigh. Despite their disagreement, she and Charlotte had cooperated in guest preparations, but Charlotte had maintained the invisible shield of sugary courtesy she employed when cross.

As if summoned by her thoughts, Charlotte appeared at her side. "Are you sure the Kleins wanted both suites? Families usually want those rooms."

"I'm sure. Bonnie said Tom gets insomnia and likes to read for hours at night. She was glad to have an adjoining room so she can get some rest." Grace smiled, remembering Bonnie's pleasant voice on the phone. It was always a good sign when their week began with friendly guests excited about their stay.

The bell above the front door chimed. They would soon find out if Bonnie's personality matched her amiable phone voice.

Grace followed Charlotte down the stairs and joined in greeting the Kleins and introducing themselves.

Bonnie had curly white hair and sparkling blue eyes. Her crisp designer outfit and artsy lavender scarf added to Grace's impression that a tiny colorful bird would be perching in their inn for a while.

Bonnie clasped her hands as she regarded the graceful stairway, the tall ceiling, and the chandelier. "Oh my. The pictures on your website are lovely, but they don't do this entry justice. If the rest of the inn is this spectacular, it may be the prettiest B and B we've ever visited." She turned to her husband. "Don't you think?"

"It sure looks like it," Tom replied. He was dressed like an elite senior golfer and towered over Bonnie.

"Thank you. We want to make your stay here as special as possible." Grace registered the couple and invited them to the inn's complimentary wine, cheese, and hors d'oeuvres hour at six.

Winston, eager to greet every guest who crossed their threshold, wagged his tail as if the Kleins were his best buddies. Still, the well-trained canine kept a polite distance until Bonnie invited him over.

As Tom and Bonnie showered the happy dog with attention, Grace said, "That's Winston. He enjoys making new friends."

"What a sweet dog," Bonnie said.

Winston yipped as if in agreement.

Everyone laughed.

Grace glanced at their stylish, oversize totes and spotted a pair of knitting needles poking out of the top of the nearest one. So Bonnie was a knitter. Winnie's forte was sewing, but she loved all crafts. Lydia Walkerton, a guest due later this evening, might not arrive in time for hospitality hour. With no other visitors to boost conversation, Grace decided to call her aunt and invite her over to make a new friend.

"I'd love to," Winnie said. "And I'll bring a cherry pie."

After Grace thanked her aunt and disconnected, the tall grandfather clock in the foyer struck three.

"Nice clock you got there," Tom said. "It might be about the same age as my grandfather's watch." He pulled a gold antique watch from his pocket and flipped it open, smiling proudly. "I'd rather carry this than wear an expensive new watch any day."

Grace and Charlotte exclaimed over its fine craftsmanship.

Charlotte offered to help Tom carry their luggage upstairs, as he appeared to be a bit older than Bonnie.

He brushed aside her offer with a smile. "You'd think my doctor would take it easier on an old guy, but he'll be really happy to know I'm hauling Bonnie's stuff up and down the stairs."

Bonnie rolled her eyes as she motioned to the two enormous suitcases they'd brought in. "Tom makes it sound like I brought a dozen trunks." She grinned at her husband. "After all, we're staying for a while. I need something to wear. Though I suppose you can leave the rest of the luggage in the car. I can buy what I need while we're here."

"No more new clothes." Tom hastily grabbed one of the suitcases and trailed Charlotte upstairs to their suites.

Chuckling as she watched them ascend, Grace wondered if hospitality hour without any other men to talk to might be a bit much for Tom. Maybe Spencer Lewis, their neighbor, would respond to a last-minute invite, especially if it involved Winnie's cherry pie and Charlotte's delicious creations.

Spencer, a widower with a lean, athletic physique and salt-and-pepper hair, exuded a strong, quiet attractiveness. Grace liked the way he'd embraced country life after an intense career as an FBI intelligence analyst—a past he preferred to downplay.

Since his move to Magnolia Harbor, Spencer had been neighborly, dropping in and helping with the heavy lifting. Occasionally, Grace and Charlotte had thanked him with dinner at the inn. Grace regularly saw Spencer around town and always enjoyed his company at social events.

Grace hit speed dial.

"Hey, Grace." Spencer's deep voice made her smile. "What can I do for you?"

"I wondered if you'd like to come over for wine and cheese this evening. And Winnie's cherry pie."

"You know I'm not going to turn down Winnie's pie."

"Well, now that you're hooked, I'll tell you my ulterior motive," Grace confessed. "A new couple has arrived, and the husband could use another man to talk to. Otherwise, he'll be stuck with a veranda full of X chromosomes."

Spencer chuckled. "I'll bet the guy won't mind being surrounded by lovely ladies, but if you want me to come, I'll be glad to supply a Y."

Charlotte

Charlotte sat at the front desk, waiting for their guest Lydia Walkerton to arrive. Grace was the people person in their partnership, but Charlotte also believed the "hospitality" in their hospitality hour meant more than just exceptional food.

She checked the time and winced. She'd calculated the exact moment when her spicy chorizo cheese balls should come out of the oven, outer crusts crisp but not too crisp, and it was only twelve minutes away.

Hopefully, Lydia would appear in time for Charlotte to remove the appetizers from the oven, take care of last-minute details, and arrange the food on the veranda.

Underneath her concerns, a small inner voice prodded her about the Great Caviar Controversy. Despite their cooperation, the conflict still caused tension between her and Grace.

And be kind to one another, tenderhearted, forgiving one another, even as God in Christ forgave you. The Bible verse, spoken in her mother's gentle tone, echoed through Charlotte's mind.

Their mother had never let Charlotte and Grace forget the verse, especially when they clashed. Carrying on the legacy, Grace had hung up an intricate antique sampler in the kitchen hallway that bore those words.

Charlotte fiddled with her phone, staring at the front door and willing it to open.

It finally did. A chic woman in her fifties with dark hair and dark circles under her eyes entered, pulling sleek luggage on wheels.

Charlotte smiled. "Good evening, and welcome to our inn. I'm Charlotte Wylde, one of the owners. Are you Lydia Walkerton?"

The traveler nodded, as if talking took too much energy.

"Did you have a problem with your flight?" Charlotte asked.

"No," Lydia answered, sounding defensive. "I needed a little time to . . . collect things. I'm sorry I'm so late."

Charlotte silently admonished herself. She'd already broken her sister's first rule of hospitality: always make the guest feel comfortable. "There's no need to apologize. You're not late at all. In fact, you're right on time for our complimentary wine and cheese hour on the veranda."

Lydia shook her head.

"The view of the lake is lovely," Charlotte said, "especially when you've been cooped up in a plane. And maybe a little something to eat might hit the spot."

"I suppose so," Lydia said. "I forgot to eat lunch."

To Charlotte, such an omission was tantamount to forgetting to breathe. She might consume a small lunch in the interest of her waistline, but how could someone overlook eating altogether?

Smothering her surprise, Charlotte offered, "I'll be serving a variety of cheeses, wines, and fruits." She assumed Lydia's stomach couldn't handle spicy chorizo cheese balls, so she didn't mention them. Instead, she said, "This morning I made French bread. I'll top it with ricotta cheese and fresh tomatoes from our garden and add a touch of mild, homemade pesto. Does any of that sound good?"

For the first time, Lydia's nod was accompanied by a small smile. "I might attend."

"Wonderful. Feel free to join us whenever you like." Charlotte pointed the way to the veranda, then handed Lydia the key to the Buttercup Suite. "Let me help you carry your luggage upstairs."

"Thank you, but I can do it." Picking up her bags, Lydia ascended the stairs to her room.

Despite the suitcases, the woman moved with the graceful confidence of a runway model. Yet Lydia seemed anything but assured. The weary frown had returned, and Charlotte doubted she would come to hospitality hour.

While Charlotte enjoyed socializing, she didn't feel confident in this role of dealing with troubled guests. She'd detected Lydia's New York accent, yet Charlotte hadn't thought of conversing about the Big Apple, where she'd visited her cookbook publisher, until after the guest had disappeared.

How did Grace relate to their guests so effortlessly?

Charlotte hurried to the fragrant kitchen, where she felt most comfortable. She threw open the oven. The chorizo cheese balls needed a few more minutes to brown.

In the meantime, Charlotte removed the colorful plates of cheeses and watermelon-star fruit combos from the fridge and carried them to the veranda, where Grace was chatting with the Kleins.

Bonnie flashed a guilty smile at Charlotte. "I hope you don't mind our coming a few minutes early, but a glass of wine sounded so good."

Charlotte was glad she had set up the beverage table earlier, so the wines were well chilled. She preferred when guests waited until she'd finished arranging all the food and drinks, but how could anyone take offense to the friendly elderly couple? "No problem."

Tom gazed heavenward. "Bonnie likes to get her way, in case you hadn't noticed."

Charlotte and Grace laughed, and Bonnie playfully swatted her husband's arm.

"Would you care for fruit or cheese?" Charlotte asked as she set the plates on a long tray of ice her sister had apparently brought.

Tom and Bonnie took their plates and began to help themselves.

Charlotte went back to the kitchen. She removed the delicately browned chorizo cheese balls from the oven and inhaled the delicious aroma. Then she slid the cheese balls onto a hand-painted plate, set the plate on a wicker platter, and zipped to the veranda.

Only one more plate to arrange. Charlotte returned to the kitchen and sliced part of her French loaf. She spread pieces with creamy ricotta, topping each appetizer with cherry tomatoes and pesto made from herbs she'd picked that morning. Simple and delicious. So decorative too, next to the fruit and cheeses.

After surveying the veranda, Charlotte exhaled. Everything had come together quite well. The Japanese lanterns and the bamboo centerpiece appeared elegant yet casual. Grace had helped her bring out drinks and dishes and helped her arrange everything. She had folded brightly colored napkins so they resembled tropical birds alongside artistic groupings of wineglasses, plates, and silverware.

"Everything looks wonderful," Grace whispered to Charlotte.

"This is what I call true hospitality." Tom grinned and took a bite of a cheese ball.

Bonnie echoed his delight.

Charlotte smiled at her sister. She and Grace complemented each other's talents, even if they occasionally got under each other's skin.

"What a beautiful table." Winnie, bearing a large pie keeper, hugged Charlotte, then Grace as if it had been days since she'd seen them instead of mere hours.

"I'm so glad you made it," Grace said.

Charlotte nodded. "And thanks for bringing a dessert."

Winnie removed the lid, revealing a cherry pie with a flaky, golden crust. It looked incredible.

Charlotte carefully took the pie from her aunt and rearranged the table to accommodate the dessert.

Grace guided Winnie over to Tom and Bonnie, weaving their sewing and knitting interests into her introductions. Soon Winnie and Bonnie were chatting like old friends. Charlotte was surprised to learn that Tom also knitted.

"When you hand him a scarf or an afghan pattern, he's faster than I am," Bonnie admitted. "But we usually knit hats, socks, and baby sweaters for homeless shelters and pregnancy care centers. So I beat him most of the time."

No wonder the couple had brought two big totes full of knitting. Charlotte watched the threesome settle at one of the tables with their refreshments. They oohed and aahed at the gorgeous view of Lake Haven. The water sparkled brilliantly in the early evening sunshine.

With the guests occupied, Grace wandered back to Charlotte, and they each took a sliver of Winnie's pie.

Keeping her voice low, Grace said, "So Lydia Walkerton showed up?"

"Yes." Matching her sister's tone, Charlotte cut the point of her slice. "I think she was exhausted this evening, so I'm not sure if she'll join us." She took a bite and imagined that even Lydia would perk up at a taste of this delectable pie.

"Did she say why she came to Magnolia Harbor?" Grace asked.

"No," Charlotte said, then grinned. "But I'm sure you'll get it out of her."

Her sister wrinkled her nose before heading back to Winnie and the Kleins. She paused halfway, her gaze fixed on the backyard.

Spencer approached the veranda with his long stride and aimed a smile directly at Grace.

Charlotte could have sworn her sister blushed. It was all she could do to hold in a giggle.

Winston, bribed earlier with a dog biscuit to remain content outside, enthusiastically greeted their newest guest.

Spencer reached down and scratched the dog behind the ears.

"Thanks for coming, Spencer," Grace said. She gestured toward the refreshments table. "Please enjoy."

"I sure will. Thanks for having me over." Spencer turned to Charlotte. "How are you?"

"I'm warm, but it's August, isn't it?" Charlotte said. Thank goodness for ceiling fans, sending breezes across the veranda on this sultry evening.

Spencer helped himself to a generous slice of Winnie's pie, then sighed. "I just spotted your chorizo cheese balls." He extended his plate to Grace. "Do you want half of this piece of pie?"

"Goodness, no. I already had some." She scooted away from him.

"I already ate mine too." Charlotte held up both hands. "We're counting on you to eat at least two slices."

Spencer grinned. "I'll do my best."

"When you've filled your plate, let me introduce you to the rest of our guests," Grace told him.

He stepped toward her. "I'd better go over there now, or I'll end up taking the whole spread with me."

When Grace and Spencer joined the group, Winnie and Bonnie paused their conversation about crafts. Grace made the introductions.

Soon Winnie and Bonnie resumed their lively conversation, and Spencer and Tom started talking about their favorite travel destinations.

As they all chatted, Charlotte glanced at her sister. Grace seemed to be relaxing, and her small smile bloomed.

To Charlotte's surprise, Lydia appeared on the veranda. She looked as if she hadn't rested a minute since her arrival. In fact, her red eyes indicated that she'd probably been crying. What in the world was bothering her? Charlotte cringed inwardly. *Lord, what if she can't hold back? You know I don't do well with crying.*

But she did do well with food. Charlotte picked up the cheese plate and approached Lydia. "We're so glad you're joining us."

"Thank you." Lydia brightened a little at the sight of the hors d'oeuvres.

"Please help yourself," Charlotte urged.

"I love Brie and Gruyère," Lydia said, taking a piece of cheese. "Especially with a good pinot noir."

"Coming right up." Charlotte set the plate down and poured a glass.

Lydia sipped the wine and sampled the cheese. Her tight face relaxed. "Wonderful."

Surprisingly, Lydia thawed enough to talk about various cheese-and-wine pairings—a subject Charlotte could discuss all night.

Charlotte remembered to bring up New York and found herself enjoying their conversation. Lydia, who designed clothes such as her own conservative but fashionable dress, had eaten at all of Charlotte's favorite restaurants in the city.

Lydia was talking about her favorite Broadway shows when Grace approached them. Charlotte introduced her sister to Lydia.

Grace smiled at their guest. "You really must meet our aunt Winnie."

Charlotte almost hated to end her conversation with Lydia, but the woman needed to become acquainted with the others. Maybe more connections would result in fun activities with them, taking her mind off her troubles.

Winnie and Bonnie seemed to pick up on Lydia's trouble too, because they immediately joined forces to make the younger woman feel at home. Before long, Winnie had invited both women to a session with The Busy Bees, her quilting group.

After a few minutes, Charlotte headed for the refreshments table. The heat hadn't subsided in the least, so she wanted to make sure the fruit still looked fresh and the cheeses weren't turning gooey.

She stopped dead in her tracks at the sight of an uninvited guest. Dean Bradley.

He wore a navy shirt and tailored chinos, and he was inspecting her food with a slight smile.

"Well, I do declare," Charlotte teased, thickening her Southern accent. "If it isn't the actual Dean Bradley, owner of the acclaimed inn The Tidewater, on the wrong side of the lake to grace us with his presence. I do hope you find something palatable among our meager offerings."

"What a great evening for hors d'oeuvres on the veranda." Dean poured a full glass of her most expensive wine, scanning the refreshments with an appreciative eye. "And such artistic presentation. You always could take simple ingredients and make them special."

"Thank you." Charlotte gestured to the glass in his hand. "You always did have taste."

"Don't you think a few sheep cheeses might complete this tray?" he asked.

Charlotte rolled her eyes. "You can add sheep cheeses when you do your own tray." Why did she let him annoy her? She took a long, slow breath as she fussed with the table.

"Dean, it's good to see you," Grace said, sweeping in with her most gracious smile. Apparently, she'd caught Charlotte's strident tone from across the veranda. "You haven't met our guests yet." She ushered him toward Bonnie and Lydia and made the introductions.

"Let's talk about Candlelight weekend," Winnie said. She turned to Charlotte. "Tell us about your party. What are you making to eat?"

"I'm not quite sure yet," Charlotte hedged. After her tiff with

Grace about the food, she wasn't in the mood to discuss it. Even less so with her main culinary rival privy to the conversation.

"If you need any ideas, I could give you some suggestions," Dean said eagerly. "At Le Cordon Bleu, I learned a dozen exclusive recipes featuring sturgeon caviar, which I think is an absolute must. The salmon caviar is fine but not quite right. Don't you agree?"

How could the man zero in on the worst possible subject this evening? Charlotte gritted her teeth as he went on to describe a handful of recipes he'd learned at the prestigious culinary school. She couldn't help but notice that Grace's lips were pressed thin, a sure sign that she wasn't pleased either.

"Hey, Dean, come over here and take a load off," Spencer called.

Charlotte stifled a sigh of relief as their neighbor drew Dean into the conversation. Maybe Dean would get so busy talking to Spencer and Tom that he'd forget about sharing more recipes.

Fortunately, the rest of the social hour went smoothly. The Kleins and Lydia eventually excused themselves and went up to their suites, and Winnie headed home, leaving only Spencer and Dean.

"Let's get this food and wine put away," Charlotte said.

Dean helped Charlotte carry the plates and bottles to the kitchen while Grace and Spencer took the dirty dishes and glasses.

Charlotte put the remaining food in the fridge, and Grace tidied up the kitchen.

"Would you like me to do the dishes to make up for my rudeness in arriving unannounced and empty-handed?" Dean asked, his unfairly gorgeous eyes twinkling.

"That won't be necessary," Charlotte said with a haughty sniff. "I'm sure you'll break something."

"I'd better get back to The Tidewater then," Dean said with a grin. "Thanks for a lovely evening."

"I'd better go too," Spencer said. "Thank you for the delicious food and great company."

"I'm glad you both came," Grace said.

"Charlotte, let me know if you want those sturgeon recipes," Dean said over his shoulder as he left with Spencer.

Charlotte froze midwave.

After the door closed, Grace took one look at Charlotte and burst out laughing.

Charlotte couldn't help but join in, and she laughed until her sides hurt.

"Sometimes Dean can't read a room," Grace said.

"But he can be nice," Charlotte conceded, remembering how he'd forgiven some of her past hasty judgments. If only he didn't press her buttons sometimes.

"You were very nice too." Grace hugged her. "I was proud of how you managed it. Sometimes I forget to thank you for all you do for our business."

Basking in her sister's appreciation, Charlotte smiled. "You're the one who makes our guests feel at home and keeps everything running like a well-oiled machine. I just do the food."

"Come on," Grace said. "You do much more than that."

"You're right," Charlotte teased as she started loading the dishwasher. "I do the dishes too."

They both laughed.

When their laughter died down, Grace turned serious. "I'm sorry about earlier."

"Me too," Charlotte said, squeezing her hand.

"So I've been thinking about Candlelight weekend," Grace said hesitantly. "And I've decided that you're right about the party."

Charlotte gaped at her. She didn't know what to say.

"The fact that Dean agreed with you without even knowing it cinched it for me. It's the perfect opportunity to strut our stuff, so let's go all out." Grace grinned. "But use your caviar recipes, not Dean's."

At that, laughter once again filled the kitchen.

4

Winnie

"Of course I understand," Winnie said. She breathed deeply, trying to ease her heartbeat thundering in her ears, then managed a slow, deliberate goodbye.

She ached to hurl her cell phone against the wooden front door, but her grandchildren, playing with water blasters out by the blooming myrtles, would hear and come running to see what was the matter.

But she wanted them to come running. Grandbaby hugs wouldn't make it all better, but they'd help.

Winnie went inside and opened the freezer, welcoming its cold breath on her face. She excavated homemade strawberry ice pops from piles of frozen pork chops, black-eyed peas, and okra. She walked to the front steps and held up the treats. "Want some ice pops?" she called to her grandchildren.

Seven-year-old Sam and five-year-old Monica came dashing toward her with love in their eyes.

Winnie didn't mind sharing their affection with ice pops. Her grandchildren had already brightened this awful morning. Gus, her retired husband, always made her feel better, but he was gone for the day.

"Hello," Grace called. She got out of her car and waved at Winnie and the children from the driveway. Her niece looked as fresh as a flower despite the heat.

"Good morning." A moment or two with Grace on the porch

swing would help her feel better too. Winnie shooed the kids into the yard with their drippy treats, then asked Grace, "Want an ice pop?"

"Sounds great, but I'd dribble it all over your porch and my clothes."

Winnie sat on the swing and patted the seat beside her. Grace joined her aunt, and they started swinging.

Phoebe, her green-eyed tabby cat, who had hidden at the first sign of the water wars, sneaked out from under the porch and leaped onto Winnie's lap.

She stroked the cat, trying to let Phoebe's contented purrs calm her down.

Grace cocked her head. "How are you doing today?"

Winnie grimaced. Her niece had already picked up on her mood. "Well, I've been better."

"It must be a dilly if Monica and Sam can't fix it." Grace leaned toward her. "What's going on?"

"It's that town council." Winnie couldn't stop the words any more than she could stop a thunderstorm. "They've gone and hired an intern to run the Candlelight Journey Festival."

Grace raised her eyebrows. "I'd heard they're paying Jillian Price to handle the details this year. She's the mayor's niece. But what does that have to do with you?"

"It has everything to do with me!" Winnie burst out. "And it's not only me. Jillian doesn't know what she's doing. She'll mess up the whole festival!"

Grace blinked. Phoebe leaped down and hid under the porch again. Even the grandchildren stopped eating their treats and stared at her.

Shame on me. Winnie forced a smile at the kids. "It's all right. Silly Grandma's just pitching a hissy fit."

They giggled a little uncertainly but returned to their refreshments.

"What's wrong?" Grace asked gently. "What has Jillian done?"

Keeping her voice low, Winnie said, "You know how I'm in charge of the greeters?"

Grace nodded.

"Well, this morning, Jillian called and informed me that I can take this year off."

Grace blinked again. "Why? You've headed up the greeters for years."

"Probably twice as long as she's been on this earth." Sourness crept into Winnie's throat. "But that's not all."

"What else?" Grace asked, regarding her aunt with sympathetic blue eyes.

Winnie had to breathe slowly to keep the sobs inside. Finally, she said, "Jillian told me she doesn't need me to make costumes this year."

"What?" Grace blurted out.

Now Winnie had to caution her niece to hold down her volume.

"Does she think the Candlelight Journey soldiers are going to wear jeans and T-shirts?" Grace asked in a fierce whisper.

"Blue T-shirts for our side and red ones for the redcoats." Winnie's sad laugh ended in a smothered sob. "You and I know that actor turnover every year means new costumes have to be made. Plus, Jillian has come up with a Revolutionary War play, so they'll need even more costumes."

"What did Patty say about all this?" Grace asked, referring to festival committee member Patty Duncan. She was also Winnie's friend and a fellow member of The Busy Bees quilting group.

"I heard Patty's excited about it—not that she's called me lately," Winnie said. She couldn't keep her voice from trembling. "I haven't heard from her since Jillian came to town."

Lines furrowed Grace's smooth forehead. "Patty does love drama, doesn't she? But she's your friend, and she's sewn with you for years.

She realizes how much you contribute to the festival. I would think she'd tell Jillian how valuable you are."

"Apparently, she hasn't," Winnie said. It seemed like Patty had forgotten she existed. "Who will make all those extra costumes?"

Grace took Winnie's hand and gave it a comforting squeeze.

As Winnie fought tears, she glanced at Sam and Monica, who had finished their ice pops. Thankfully, they were playing with their water blasters again and didn't seem to notice their grandmother's mood. Still, Winnie didn't want to upset them, so she ushered her niece into the cool, pleasant living room.

Winnie dropped onto the comfortable sofa. Grace sat beside her and encircled her in a hug while she cried.

When her sobs faded to hiccups, Grace went into the kitchen and returned with ice pops and two of Winnie's older dish towels. "I know this is breaking the rules."

"But drastic times call for drastic measures," Winnie said.

Grace smiled as she handed her aunt an ice pop and a towel, then sat down next to her on the sofa again.

Winnie spread the dish towel across her knees and bit into the frosty, tangy treat. "This is just right. Good for beestings when my girls were little. Good for breakups when they got big." She steadied her voice. "I guess they're just as good for grandmas when they're hurting."

"You bet." Grace patted her shoulder.

When they'd finished the treats and wiped away every trace of juice, Grace said, "Feel a little better?"

Winnie tried to smile. "Well, just because I've made the costumes since forever, this news is not the end of the world."

"You and Mama made them together when I was a little girl. I loved the blue dress and pretty cap you two made for me when I was nine. I still have it."

Winnie knew that dear Grace meant to bring back pleasant memories, but recalling her late sister, Hazel, threatened a new set of sniffles. Winnie clung to the mental picture of her darling niece in that frock, long brown braids poking out of the lacy mobcap. "You were the perfect little festival actress. Kept that dress as clean as the day we finished it."

They traveled down memory lane for a little while, and the heat in Winnie's cheeks dropped a few degrees. But white-hot flames still licked inside her stomach.

"I'd better check on the children," Winnie said, getting up. When she peeked out the door, she noticed that they had abandoned their water blasters and were now taking a break on the porch swing.

She returned to the living room and took her seat on the sofa. "I still can't believe I won't be making costumes this year."

"Did you ask Jillian how she came to this decision?" Grace asked slowly. "Did you tell her how it would affect the festival?"

"What do you mean?" Winnie said.

"Tourists love your designs, and it's one big reason why they come," Grace explained. "The town will lose revenue if Jillian uses cheap substitutes. Because she's not going to find anyone like you to sew and fit all those costumes—not in our time frame and certainly not for free."

"Maybe after forking out big bucks to pay her and whoever she lines up, the town council will come to their senses," Winnie muttered. "Maybe you're right. I should talk to Jillian about it." But that was the last thing she felt like doing.

Winnie's daughter Paisley arrived to pick up her kids. Fortunately, she was in too big of a hurry to notice Winnie's forced smile. Grace said she needed to get back to the inn, and they left Winnie to come up with her own solution.

If there was one.

Winnie sighed. It was only Tuesday, and she'd already piled up a heap of sins. She had a sneaking suspicion she wouldn't get over this by sundown or even by sundown Saturday. She loved Sundays, but how could she drag a mess like this through the church doors?

She retreated to the porch and flopped onto the swing again.

Brave Phoebe reappeared, rubbing against Winnie's ankles.

"If I were you, I'd go back under the porch," Winnie warned her.

Instead, with a small meow, the cat jumped onto her lap once more. *You rescued me*, she seemed to say. *Now it's my turn to rescue you.*

Cuddling her pet, Winnie stared at the dozens of brilliantly colored zinnias that surrounded her porch. How long the pair sat there, she didn't know, but when she heard the clock chime from the living room, she told Phoebe she'd better start supper soon.

Phoebe obliged by trotting to the backyard to chase butterflies.

As Winnie headed into the house, she thought about The Busy Bees meeting that night and felt a sense of dread. She couldn't remember another Tuesday evening when she hadn't looked forward to quilting with her friends.

There's always a first time for everything, I suppose.

Winnie wasn't sure if she could face Patty right now. Her friend had missed the last couple of meetings, but would she show up tonight?

Winnie glared in the hall mirror. More gray hair seemed to appear every day. She smoothed, then smacked a stray lock of dark blonde hair that wouldn't behave.

"Hey, hey, what's this? Be nice to my gal." Gus, coming up behind her, stroked her head with a calloused hand and smiled.

"Don't try to sweet-talk me, Gus Bennett." She attempted to glare at him too, but her anger was already ebbing. Her high school sweetheart and husband of nearly fifty years could still wield the charming smile that had won her heart so long ago.

"Why don't you relax?" Gus said. "Go have a good time with the ladies, like you always do."

Winnie remained silent.

"You don't even know Patty's coming tonight," he reminded her.

"She'll be there just to spite me," she mumbled.

Gus sighed. "This isn't like you. You're talking about Patty, right? Patty, who's been your friend for years."

"If she really was a friend, she would have stuck up for me." Winnie crossed her arms over her chest. "Or at least she'd call me."

"You need to calm down if you're going to take the inn guests with you to the meeting," he said.

She frowned. If only she hadn't invited Bonnie Klein and Lydia Walkerton to join them. "Only Bonnie accepted my invitation. But we can't have her feel unwelcome." Every Southern bone in her body rebelled at the thought.

"That sure wouldn't do Grace and Charlotte's inn any good," Gus remarked.

Winnie wished he wasn't right. "Okay. I'll make Bonnie feel so welcome that she'll want to move here. But I'm never going to speak to you-know-who again."

He gave her a reproachful look.

She grabbed her quilting tote and strode out of the house, not daring to glance back. The August heat and humidity still wrapped around her like a soggy, wet blanket. She got into her car and cranked up the air-conditioning. The short drive to the inn cooled her insides a little.

Winnie said hello to Charlotte, then accepted the blessed bottle of chilled water Grace offered.

A few minutes later, Winnie, Grace, and Bonnie hopped into Winnie's car and left for Spool & Thread, the fabric shop where the quilting group met. Grace was not a regular member of the group, but she was helping with their latest project.

Their conversation on the way to town proved so pleasant that Winnie considered the possibility that she might survive the evening.

Judith Mason, the leader of the quilting group and owner of Spool & Thread, greeted them with her usual smile. She had gray hair and flawless dark skin.

After Winnie introduced Bonnie, Judith adjusted her glasses and gestured to a cozy grouping of chairs and sofas. "Please have a seat until the others arrive."

Grace and Bonnie sat down on a sofa.

Winnie dropped into one of the comfy chairs and fanned herself. She was more tired than she'd realized. *Getting mad takes too much energy to be worth it.*

Her feet tingled as she glanced at the door. Maybe she could still leave before Patty arrived.

Judith took bolts of Christmas material from a nearby cart and loaded Winnie's lap with them. "Isn't this some of the cutest material you've ever seen?"

Winnie was now anchored to the chair, and she couldn't walk out of the shop even if she wanted to. Did Judith know more than she was saying?

Everyone talked about holiday crafts until Helen Daley and Angel Diaz, two other members of the quilting group, walked into the shop.

"Good evening, ladies," Helen said, smoothing her chin-length blonde bob. The friendly wife of the police captain had rheumatoid arthritis, but it didn't stop her from doing the hobbies she enjoyed.

"It's great to see everyone," Angel said. The youngest member of the group, she was a talented artist who experimented in a variety of mediums. She also worked part-time at the Dragonfly Coffee Shop nearby.

Winnie introduced Bonnie to the newcomers, and they all took their seats at the sewing machines and resumed their current project.

Winnie and Bonnie ended up at neighboring machines, so Winnie explained that they were working on baby quilts for the hospital and showed her the available material.

"Nowadays many young mothers like funky color schemes," Bonnie commented. She paired dinosaur prints with black, green, orange, and red blocks.

"Good choices," Winnie said, even though she preferred the more traditional pastel stripes, polka dots, flowers, and cuddly animals for babies. She was making a pastel quilt with teddy bears on it.

Before Winnie knew it, she and Bonnie were working together as if they'd done it every week.

For a while, Winnie stitched away with no knots in her thread and only an occasional one in her stomach.

Until Patty walked in.

Winnie glanced up, then away.

"Sorry I'm late," Patty announced to the quilters. "I lost track of time. I've been so busy lately."

Too busy to be a friend. "It was nice of you to show up anyway. Even if you're late, I'm glad you get to meet my new friend." Winnie introduced her to Bonnie.

"It's wonderful to meet you," Bonnie said.

"You too." Patty gestured to Bonnie's vibrant materials. "Oh, I love your color scheme."

Winnie sat quietly as Patty and Bonnie discussed their quilts.

Grace, sitting at a nearby machine, hadn't missed a trick. Her eyes begged Winnie to be civil.

She couldn't escape the times she'd counseled her niece to live and let live. Despite the thick, invisible wall between her and Patty, Winnie had almost decided to heed her own advice—at least for the evening.

But then Patty stopped by her sewing machine and said, "Jillian and I have been talking, and we realized we'll need more help after all."

Winnie blinked. They'd come to their senses? For a second, she toyed with the idea of turning them down. They definitely deserved it. But out of the goodness of her heart, she'd say yes—

"We've decided to include you on the cleanup committee," Patty said matter-of-factly.

Her words exploded inside Winnie like grenades.

Before Winnie could respond, Judith clapped to get everyone's attention. "Why don't we all take a break? I have homemade apple-cinnamon doughnuts and coffee over there." She pointed to a refreshments table, then ushered Patty toward it.

The others got up and went over to the table. They talked about the Candlelight Journey Festival, carefully avoiding any references to costumes. Or to cleanup.

Dazed, Winnie remained seated at her sewing machine.

Grace's hand pressed both understanding and a warning into her shoulder. *Don't get into it. Not yet.*

For her niece's sake—especially with an inn guest present—Winnie didn't.

When the others returned to their work, Winnie pleaded a headache, and it wasn't a fib. Sledgehammers seemed to slam her forehead.

Normally, nothing would have stopped Winnie from finishing a project, especially when the group had agreed to finish the baby quilts within two weeks. She'd never leave a guest she'd invited either, not even with Grace, who would apologize for her. Winnie's mama had taught her better manners than that.

However, tonight was anything but normal.

After Grace assured her that she and Bonnie would get a ride back to the inn, Winnie murmured a goodbye to the others. She slipped out of the cheerful shop and into the shadowy twilight. A single star glimmered feebly through murky clouds.

Winnie knew neither she nor the star was alone.

But that didn't keep her from feeling lonely tonight.

5

Grace

"How did The Busy Bees meeting go last night?" Charlotte asked as she cooked bacon, eggs, and cheese grits for their guests.

Sighing, Grace told her about the tension between Winnie and Patty. "Winnie was so upset that she left early," she concluded.

"That's terrible," Charlotte remarked. "And it's so unlike Winnie."

"I know." Grace pushed a tendril of hair behind her ear. She was already tired this morning, so she was glad the other guests weren't expected to arrive until three. Maybe she'd have a little time to rest before then.

As Charlotte placed the food on plates, Grace retrieved the silverware, glasses, and napkins. Then they carried everything to the dining room.

"Looks like we're just in time," Tom said as he entered the room with Bonnie.

Grace smiled. "Hope you both slept well."

"Never better," Bonnie replied. "It's so comfortable and peaceful here. I think even Tom got a few hours in."

Right after Tom and Bonnie took their seats, Lydia walked in.

"Good morning," Charlotte said brightly.

Lydia nodded and sat down across from Bonnie.

As their guests chatted and ate their breakfast, Grace munched a piece of crisp bacon. She mixed her eggs and grits together, then scooped up a big forkful.

The bell above the front door chimed.

Who could that be? They weren't expecting anyone this early. "I'll go see who it is," Grace said. She hurried to the foyer.

A tall man stood at the front desk. Despite the heat, he wore a dark beret, a long cape, and leather knee-high boots. Looking as if he'd stepped out of a castle portrait, he cut a striking figure. An old-fashioned trunk sat at his feet.

"Welcome to Magnolia Harbor Inn," she said, smiling. "I'm Grace Porter."

Winston trotted over to investigate the visitor. He wagged and whined as if he couldn't wait to meet him.

"And this is Winston," Grace said. "He enjoys meeting new people."

Forgetting his usual good manners, Winston nosed the man's knees.

The man bent down and petted the dog with nearly equal enthusiasm. "You're a fine fellow, Winston. I know we shall be friends."

"You must be Dr. Ian Southby," Grace said, still surprised to see him here so early. She always informed guests that arrival time was three o'clock unless other arrangements were made.

Ian nodded, then glanced around the foyer. "What a truly magnificent entrance." He circled the area, studying the cathedral ceiling, the elegant stairway, the chandelier that glistened in the morning sunlight. They seemed to have struck him speechless. Finally, he asked, "This mansion was built in the early 1800s, wasn't it?"

"In 1816," Grace answered.

He examined the wrought iron balustrade. "I imagine this came from another country. Perhaps England?"

Grace blinked. "As a matter of fact, it did. According to a letter we found in the attic, the house's first mistress wanted something more elaborate than what local ironworkers could produce at that time."

With Winston at his heels, Ian murmured to himself as he wandered from wall to wall, then down the hallway toward the kitchen.

Grace followed, not quite sure what to do or say. She'd never seen a guest scrutinize the inn like this before.

Ian stopped dead in his tracks. "What a marvelous sampler."

"Thank you. It's one of my favorite antiques." The sampler he indicated, with its intricate green, gold, and cream needlework, had been a lucky flea market find. The Bible verse stitched on it had been one of her mother's favorites. And it was a good daily reminder to be kind and forgiving.

He hovered within inches of the sampler. "Do you know its age?"

She'd always meant to research it, but she had never found the time. "No, but I imagine Elizabeth Byrd, the fourteen-year-old girl who signed the sampler, sewed it sometime during the 1800s."

"Amazing how young girls could display such patience in their art." Ian began to describe fascinating samplers he'd encountered in his travels.

It was interesting, but Grace's long to-do list this morning did not include an hour-long guest registration. "Excuse me, but I do need to confirm your information before issuing you a room key. You are from Springfield, Illinois, right?"

"Yes, I am," he answered. "I teach history at a university there."

"That does not surprise me in the least," Grace said as she led him back to the front desk. She retrieved his room key and slipped it into her pocket. "If you're interested, breakfast is currently being served in the dining room."

"Thank you, but I've already eaten," Ian said. "I would greatly appreciate a tour of the mansion and its grounds if you'd be so kind."

"I'm so sorry, but I can only direct you to your room and give you a quick overall picture of the property this morning." Grace summarized its layout and the inn's amenities, then said, "I'll be able to give you a tour after lunch. You're also welcome to explore on your own."

"I understand," Ian said, lifting the large trunk with ease. "Lead on."

As Grace ushered him to his room, she marveled at his strength. How did he carry that trunk up the stairs with only a pause or two? And he appeared to stop only to point out something in the decor. When they reached the Wisteria Loft Suite on the third floor, he wasn't even breathing hard.

She unlocked the door and held it open as he took the trunk inside and set it down.

"What a charming suite." Dr. Southby spread his long arms like wings and circled the room as he had the foyer. "The headboard, the furniture, the fireplace—such artistry. Where did you find them?" Without waiting for an answer, he swooped to the French doors and opened them. "A sublime view of the lake too."

Grace pointed at the interior door. "The bathroom is through there."

"I suppose that you modernized some aspects of the building," he said, regret coloring his voice.

"Yes." *I'm sorry, but most guests prefer indoor plumbing.*

Ian exhaled deeply. "It can't be avoided. But you have preserved most of the house's authenticity quite well."

"Thank you. I'll put your key on the dresser." Grace set it there.

"I wish to thank you for your assistance," Ian said, walking over to her. He bowed over her hand.

Grace smiled and nodded, then left the room and descended the stairs.

Ian was friendly, but he also seemed a bit forward. The thought of taking a tour later—an extended tour, no doubt—of the property with the historian made her a little uneasy.

Shrugging off the feeling, she returned to the dining room. The Kleins and Lydia were gone, and Charlotte was clearing the table.

Grace helped her sister carry the empty plates and glasses to the kitchen. "I just checked in Dr. Ian Southby."

"Really?" Charlotte asked, raising her eyebrows. "He arrived early."

"Indeed." Grace told her about their quirky guest and the tour of the mansion she'd promised him.

"Good luck with that," Charlotte said with a grin.

Though Ian greeted Charlotte with extravagant pleasantries, he glued himself to Grace for the promised tour. After more than an hour of listening to the historian's monologue, only a plea that she still had to clean a bathroom sent him elsewhere.

Grace had just finished her task when the bell above the front door chimed. Had Daniel and Magdalena Sims, their honeymooning guests, arrived early too?

Grace strode to the foyer, with Winston trotting beside her.

Patty Duncan, wearing her hospital physical therapist scrubs, stood at the front desk with a young woman in her twenties. The woman had long black hair, and she wore a plain knit dress.

"Grace, I'm so glad you're home," Patty said, her green eyes sparkling. "And you too, Winston."

The dog bounded over to Patty, wagging his tail.

Patty reached down and petted him. When she straightened, she gestured to her companion. "This is Jillian Price, the new coordinator of the Candlelight Journey Festival."

So this was the intern who was going to trash their celebration, according to Winnie. Grace summoned a smile. "My, you must be one busy lady."

"Yes, there's tons to do, but it's all good." Jillian hugged herself and smiled. "I'm loving every minute of it."

For the first time, Grace felt a twinge of pity. This naive young woman had no clue that in antagonizing Winnie—and probably other longtime festival fixtures—she'd stirred up a hornet's nest.

"We're so glad to have Jillian," Patty remarked. "She's going to put us on the map."

Grace nodded. "Can I offer you both some sweet tea?"

"Thanks," Patty said.

"That would be great," Jillian added.

"Follow me," Grace said as she led them into the living room.

"What a beautiful view of the lake," Jillian gushed, gazing out the windows. Then she sat down next to Patty on one of the sofas.

Winston joined them, stretching out in the middle of the floor.

Grace went to the kitchen and poured two glasses of sweet iced tea. When she returned, she passed out the glasses and took a seat in an armchair. "How are the plans for the festival coming along?"

While Patty and Jillian told Grace about the preparations, Charlotte entered the room.

"I'm so glad to see you," Patty said. She introduced Charlotte to Jillian.

Charlotte greeted everyone and sat down on the sofa across from the guests.

Patty filled them in on Jillian's new role. "I love Jillian's innovative approach to the festival. She's added several events, including a play she wrote called *The Redcoat in Me*. It's historical."

"Sort of." Jillian flipped a curtain of hair from her eyes. "But the message is so much bigger than that. The Revolutionary War scenes alternate with portrayals of the battles our subconscious fights against marginalizing expectations . . ."

Grace tried to follow Jillian's long play summary, but it was difficult. She glanced at Charlotte and thought her sister was having a hard time too.

When Jillian finished her summary, Patty finally explained the reason for their visit. "We're trying to recruit actors for the play. There are still some meaty roles available." She smiled. "I'm playing the id."

Charlotte cocked her head. "The id from Freud's personality theory?"

Patty nodded. "Jillian wanted a free spirit to play that part. But we still need a superego and a Martha Washington."

"My goodness," Grace said. Acting wasn't her cup of tea, and she didn't want to play General Washington's wife. Never in her wildest dreams had she pictured playing a superego.

"I know it's a last-minute thing." Jillian smiled at Grace and then Charlotte. "But Patty told me how savvy and artistic you both are."

"Maybe when I'm in the kitchen, whipping up a new recipe." Charlotte shook her head. "But not speaking onstage."

Grace wasn't surprised that her sister didn't want to be in the play. Charlotte had a beautiful voice and enjoyed singing in their church choir, but she'd never coveted solo parts.

"It's always so hectic during Candlelight weekend," Grace said. "Charlotte and I have a full inn all weekend, and we'll barely have a chance to get away to enjoy the festival." She clucked her tongue regretfully. "I'm sorry, but even if we possessed a shred of acting talent between the two of us, we'd have to say no."

"I was afraid you'd be too busy," Jillian said, "but I had to try."

Grace fought the urge to offer to play Martha Washington. If the role involved the acting ability of a bush—she hadn't wanted to mention even that second-grade drama background—then she could fill in.

Charlotte seemed to read her mind. She gave Grace a warning look. Patty leaped to her feet as if on springs. "What is the matter with me? I know someone we haven't asked." She threw her arms around the downcast Jillian. "Dean Bradley will make a perfect superego."

Grace choked back a laugh, not daring to glance at Charlotte. Freud considered the superego the moral side of the human personality, but in Charlotte's mind, Dean gave the role a whole new meaning.

"You should get to know Dean. He's a great guy," Patty told Jillian. "Plus, he's going to throw the best bash this festival has ever seen."

Charlotte frowned.

Grace's mirth died.

"Everyone's talking about how great it will be," Patty babbled. "His food is to die for, and it's famous all over the South. I love his inn. It's gorgeous." She tugged Jillian to her feet. "Come on. Let's go ask him to be in the play."

"Thanks for dropping by," Grace offered lamely as she and Charlotte followed them to the door. "So nice to meet you, Jillian. We're sorry we couldn't help you."

Charlotte said nothing.

But judging from her sister's expression, Grace feared that once their visitors were out of earshot, Charlotte would have plenty to say.

6

Charlotte

Charlotte couldn't believe that Patty had claimed that Dean was throwing the best party of the festival. *And hello, I was sitting right there.*

Grace shut the front door and turned to Charlotte.

"Too bad you can't have Dean cater our party," Charlotte said, crossing her arms. "His cooking's famous all over the South, you know, and his party will be the best one that anyone has ever seen."

"Don't let Patty get to you," Grace said kindly. "I know she didn't mean to put you down. She was just excited about finding the perfect superego."

Usually Grace made Charlotte feel better, but with a writing deadline and festival preparations looming, she was a little anxious. She didn't need to worry about Patty or Dean and his fabulous party right now.

Charlotte challenged herself to focus on something positive instead. Her thoughts turned to the social hour, and she got an idea. "Tonight I'll make grilled pineapple with Havarti and bacon and garlic *piadina* with sweet peppers and leeks. And huckleberry mini-cheesecakes."

"It all sounds wonderful," Grace said. "Do you have everything you need?"

Charlotte took a mental inventory. "No, I'm missing a few things. I'll run over to Hanson's now." She checked her watch. "There's still plenty of time."

Winston yipped and danced around her feet, obviously wanting to go along.

"Sorry, boy, but you have to stay here," Charlotte said as she grabbed her purse. "I'll be back soon." She left and walked to her car.

Charlotte drove to Hanson's Farm Fresh Foods and was relieved that they had all the items she needed in stock.

When she finished her shopping, she decided to stop at the Dragonfly Coffee Shop for an afternoon pick-me-up.

The shop was empty when Charlotte entered.

Angel smiled at her from behind the counter. "What will it be today?"

"A large vanilla latte," Charlotte replied. "With whipped cream."

"Coming right up." Angel bustled around behind the counter.

"Have you been busy?" Charlotte asked.

"Most of the day was crazy." Angel glanced over her shoulder and grinned. "And I was offered a role in the festival's play."

"Let me guess. Patty and Jillian were here?"

Angel put the finishing touches on the coffee and gave the cup to Charlotte. Today her olive-skinned hands featured delicate henna tattoos. "How did you know?"

"They stopped by the inn to recruit Grace and me," Charlotte answered. "What did you say?"

"I told them I'm too busy with work." Angel chuckled. "Besides, I haven't been on a stage since I played the back end of a camel in our church's Christmas play when I was a kid."

Charlotte laughed. "We said no too."

"Would you like to sit down for a minute?" Angel asked, motioning to a table.

"Sure." When they were seated, Charlotte took a sip of her coffee and studied Angel's somber expression. "Is something wrong?"

"Did you hear about the last Busy Bees meeting?"

"You mean the tension between Winnie and Patty?"

Angel nodded. "I was just wondering how it will affect the group."

"What do you mean?" Charlotte asked.

"I told the social worker at the hospital that we'd finish several baby quilts for the obstetric unit within two weeks," Angel replied. "We're supposed to work on them again Tuesday, but what will we do if Winnie and Patty still aren't getting along?"

"I don't know. There's not much we can do."

Angel sighed. "That's what I'm afraid of."

Winnie was such a sweetheart, and Charlotte knew that her aunt cared deeply about the festival and would be glad to help wherever she was needed. If only Patty and Jillian hadn't insulted her like that.

Charlotte hoped that Winnie and Patty could mend their friendship soon—for everyone's sake.

"Oh no! What happened?" Charlotte, adding the final touches to her hospitality hour table on the veranda, gestured at Tom's heavily bandaged right hand.

He winced and shook his head. "We were eating lunch. I wasn't paying attention to what I was doing and spilled hot coffee all over my hand. Hurt like the dickens."

Grace hurried over. "Is there anything we can do to help?"

"I drove him to the ER." Bonnie patted her husband's arm. "Thank goodness we weren't far from the hospital. They were very nice and took care of him right away. He rested awhile and said he was feeling much better this evening, so we decided to join you."

"Wouldn't want to miss out on this." Using his good hand, Tom loaded his plate with the grilled pineapple-bacon appetizers and huckleberry mini-cheesecakes Charlotte had whipped up.

Lydia arrived, appearing tense as usual.

Despite her husband's injury, Bonnie took the woman under her friendly wing, and soon they were chatting away.

Tom focused on his food. He seemed content to listen and nod occasionally.

Charlotte gave Grace a relieved look. After a tumultuous day—for Tom and Bonnie as well—hospitality hour had settled comfortably on the veranda like a longtime friend.

Of course, Bonnie talked more than Lydia, but the lines around the sad woman's mouth and eyes eased. She smiled and even initiated conversation a time or two.

Even Ian's theatrical entrance didn't seem to upset Lydia. She initially appeared surprised, but then a tiny twinkle appeared in her blue eyes as she watched him stride across the veranda.

"Good evening, one and all!" The historian bowed with a flourish, as if social hour were given in his honor.

While Charlotte didn't care for his drama, tall Ian, with his wavy black hair and dark eyes, was handsome in his own way. In that getup, he looked as if he had stepped out of some swashbuckling novel from the 1800s.

Her sister smiled as she introduced him to the other guests.

"I hope that's not a serious injury," Ian said when he noticed Tom's bandaged hand.

"I burned it, but I'll be fine," Tom answered. "I put my pocket watch in my left pocket, so I can still check the time."

"I trust you'll recover soon," Ian said, then turned to Grace and kissed her hand. "Thank you for inviting me to this wonderful soiree."

She appeared uncomfortable with his attention.

Charlotte tried to intervene on her behalf with offers of food and wine, but their infatuated guest refused to leave Grace's side.

Until Grace brought up the sampler that hung in the kitchen hallway. Charlotte frowned. Why would her sister mention that?

"Ah, the sampler!" A light shone in Ian's eyes as he turned to the other guests. "An excellent example of that period's textile art. Did you notice it?"

"No, but I'd love to see it," Bonnie answered. She stood, with Tom following suit.

"I'd like to check it out too," Lydia chimed in.

Charlotte was surprised by Lydia's interest in the sampler, but then she remembered their guest was a fashion designer and worked with fabrics. No wonder she wanted to take a peek at it.

Ian tried to include Grace in the group as they headed for the kitchen hallway, but she explained that she needed to remain on the veranda in case Daniel and Magdalena Sims came down for hospitality hour.

Instead, Charlotte wandered with them to the hall, where they bunched in front of the sampler.

Ian played tour guide. He really seemed to know a lot about historical textiles, pointing out the remarkable preservation of the sampler's silk thread and linen. "This sampler has obviously been well cared for."

Grace would be glad to hear that. Charlotte remembered when her sister had her flea market find carefully framed.

Ian continued his treatise, explaining the variety of stitches Elizabeth Byrd had used—queen, cross, long, and chain. Then he described the symbolism of various flowers in its diverse border and the finishing schools where young girls from upper-class families like Elizabeth's learned their art.

It was interesting, but Charlotte's thoughts drifted to social hour. This time of year, she always kept a careful eye on food and wine temperatures. Had she left sufficient food for Daniel and Magdalena if they came? Guys in their twenties tended to have healthy appetites.

While the others appeared engaged in Ian's lecture, Charlotte slipped back to the veranda. Sure enough, the athletic-looking Daniel was taking the last pineapple-bacon appetizer from the platter.

His petite, black-haired wife rolled her eyes at her husband. "Have you left any food for anyone else?"

Despite his tall frame, Daniel resembled a boy caught sneaking candy.

"No problem at all. I made plenty," Charlotte said. "It makes my day when people enjoy my cooking."

Magdalena laughed. "Well, then, you'll be very happy while we're here."

Charlotte smiled and introduced herself to the couple.

"I like people to call me Maggie," the young woman said.

After Charlotte replenished the appetizers, she and Grace chatted with the honeymooners. They had married exactly one week ago in Austin, Texas, where both had recently graduated from the University of Texas.

"We fell for each other our freshman year," Maggie said. "But we promised our parents that we'd graduate before we got married." She fixed an adoring gaze on her new husband, who was munching away. "I'd definitely do it again."

Daniel swallowed as he encircled her with a tanned, muscular arm. "You're more than worth the wait, honey." He pointed at the lake. "Looks like a good place to kayak. Glad we could finally get away from all the wedding craziness."

Maggie sighed. "Yes, it was fun, but my father couldn't understand why we wanted to go somewhere else for our honeymoon instead of staying in Austin."

Daniel said nothing but chewed harder, his blue eyes hardening.

"How did you hear about our inn?" Grace, apparently sensing tension, steered the conversation in a safe direction.

"Our friends stayed here when they were on vacation last year," Maggie answered. "They had a wonderful time."

"I'm so glad to hear it," Grace said.

Daniel, having demolished his hors d'oeuvres, returned to the refreshments table, then gently guided Maggie to a cozy corner where they could view the lake and cuddle as if the rest of the world didn't exist.

They were such a darling couple—so young and so in love.

A small sigh wafted through Charlotte as she began to clean up. She liked her life, but she'd also like to share it with someone special. So far, the right guy hadn't shown up.

The group returned from examining the sampler, interrupting her reverie.

Grace introduced the others to Daniel and Maggie, who exchanged polite hellos.

Lydia stiffened, and her eyes seemed to spark with rage. Turning her back on the newlyweds, she exchanged abrupt goodbyes with Charlotte and Grace and strode inside the inn, nose in the air as if someone had handed her the insult of the year.

Charlotte glanced at Daniel and Maggie. Thankfully, they appeared too focused on each other to notice Lydia's rude behavior.

Charlotte watched Lydia's angry retreat, then turned to meet Grace's puzzled expression.

Lydia had seemed more relaxed this evening than Charlotte had ever seen her. What in the world had made her so mad?

7

Grace

Thursday was a whirlwind of preparations for the party. To Grace's relief, Winnie stopped by the inn to lend a hand.

"Thanks for coming over," Grace said. "We really appreciate all your help."

"It's my pleasure." Winnie smiled. "I'm looking forward to the shindig."

"Speaking of tomorrow night, do you want to join me on the Candlelight Journey before the party?"

The Candlelight Journey was a walking tour of beautiful old homes, some of which had been built during the colonial era. Mostly tourists, rather than townspeople, went on the actual walk, but Grace, Charlotte, Winnie, and their friends continued the custom.

Winnie crossed her arms. "I'm not attending the festival."

"Come on," Grace coaxed. "It's a tradition. Won't you join me for even a block?"

"I'm not going, and that's final." Winnie snatched a dustcloth and marched away.

Grace sighed as she watched Winnie leave the room. It was unusual to see her aunt so upset. She hoped Winnie and Patty would be able to bridge the gap in their friendship before it was too late.

"Good morning," Spencer said. "Great weekend for the Candlelight, isn't it?"

"It certainly is," Grace said.

It was the day of the party, and the inn was quiet at the moment. Breakfast was finished, and Charlotte remained in the kitchen, pampering her sturgeon caviar. Tonight's hors d'oeuvres had to be the best. Lydia was in her room, Tom and Bonnie were sightseeing, and Daniel and Maggie were kayaking. Ian had gone for a walk, Winston happily trotting at his side.

Spencer's arrival interrupted a list of frantic details scrolling through Grace's brain. Not that she minded. "Thanks for coming over so early to help get ready for the party," she said. "I'm sure you have plenty to do at home."

Spencer's successful pecan farm kept him hopping, but he always dropped everything to pitch in when needed.

"That's what neighbors are for. I'd be glad to help you clean up tonight too." He grinned. "If I ever need to throw an open house for my business, you'd better believe I'll hit you and Charlotte up. Otherwise, my prospective customers will eat peanut butter and jelly off a card table."

She laughed. "You be sure and call on us."

"So, where do we begin?" Spencer asked.

Grace ushered him to the living room. She and Charlotte wanted a more homelike atmosphere than the barn they normally used for larger events, so they had decided to host the party inside the mansion and on the back veranda.

She scanned the room, mentally shifting its heavy furniture. Even with Spencer's assistance, who knew how long moving all this would take?

"Do you want to start with the sofa?" Spencer prompted.

How long had she been standing in the middle of the living

room, staring into space? "Sure. Let's move it over here to make room for the tables."

For the next hour, they shifted, shoved, and carried furniture to and from the living room, music room, and foyer, creating standing space around bistro tables and cozy conversation areas for guests who might want to linger.

"After this, I'll be one of the sitters, not standers," Spencer teased, wiping perspiration from his forehead.

Grace laughed. She had to disconnect her glance from his muscular, sweaty arms. Why did some people look good even after a morning of moving furniture? She didn't need a mirror to know she was a mess.

At that moment, Ian made one of his grand entrances. "Good morning again, Ms. Porter!"

"Good morning," she said.

Winston made a beeline for Grace and gave her a big doggy smile.

Ian swept his gold beret from his head and bowed over her hand. Then, with a theatrical gesture, he produced a big bouquet of scarlet roses from behind his back. "Lovely flowers for a lovely lady."

Grace had probably turned as red as the roses. "That's very nice, but hostess gifts really are not necessary."

"But you have made me feel so very welcome," Ian said.

"Thank you," she said. "I hope all my guests feel welcome."

A barely perceptible rumble sounded behind her.

Spencer.

If only she could be anywhere else. But Grace donned her best innkeeper smile and introduced Spencer as her helper this morning.

"Why didn't you ask me for assistance?" Ian clasped his hands, somewhat mangling the flowers he still clutched. "You need not have hired a mover. I would have been glad to help you."

"Grace didn't hire me," Spencer replied.

Ian raised his eyebrows. "She didn't?"

He thinks Spencer and I are dating. "Spencer is my neighbor." Grace hastened to put a gentle accent on the word. "We help each other out. And thank you for your thoughtfulness, but I would never allow a guest to move furniture. You are on vacation, remember?"

"I would never consider such pleasant occupation work," Ian said.

Despite the man's quirks, Grace had to admit that he radiated a certain gallantry, so rare in this day and age.

"I'm sure you know I've grown extremely fond of the exquisite sampler in your hallway," Ian commented, abruptly changing the subject.

Grace shook off the small spell he'd cast over her. Did Ian think she'd give it to him? "You know so much about historical textiles. Thank you for sharing your expertise with the other guests."

"It was a delight." Ian bowed again. "That evening merely whetted my desire to add the sampler to my personal collection. I would be glad to give you $1,000 for it."

Grace blinked. "My goodness. I'm sure that's a very generous price, but I cannot part with the sampler."

"Perhaps you would reconsider selling it for $1,500?" Ian's white teeth gleamed against his olive skin. He did possess a persuasive smile.

But he didn't know that the sampler had sentimental value. Grace tried to soften a firm tone with a smile. "I'm afraid the sampler isn't for sale at any price."

"I see." Ian glanced down at the roses he still held. "Would you permit me to borrow a vase so I can enjoy these in my room? It seems a sad waste of beauty to let them simply die."

"Of course. Charlotte's in the kitchen, where we store vases. I'm sure she'll be happy to loan you one." Grace congratulated herself that she'd solved the flowers dilemma without so much as touching them. And she'd successfully sent Ian elsewhere without being rude.

Winston, however, gave her a reproachful look as he followed Ian to the kitchen.

Traitor.

Grace turned to Spencer with a smile, only to encounter his blank expression, as hard to read as a closed book. "Well, you've made my morning so much easier," she said, hoping to soften his gaze. "I have only a few small things to carry in and arrange, and then Winnie and I will decorate. I can't tell you how much I appreciate your help."

"You're welcome," Spencer said. "I'll carry in those small things. Then I'd better head back to the farm."

Over her protests, Spencer carried several end tables into the foyer and set up more groupings of chairs.

"See you," Spencer said, then left. He didn't make a single neighborly reference to the party that night or seeing her then or . . . anything.

Standing at the window, she watched him depart. Grace tried to think if she'd somehow offended him. Or was she simply overthinking his departure? Spencer wasn't the overly chatty type. Sometimes men liked to keep their thoughts to themselves, especially if they had their minds on business.

A small inner voice whispered that perhaps Spencer considered Ian a rival for her attentions.

But that was ridiculous. Surely she'd made it crystal clear that she regarded Ian as only a guest. Besides, Spencer was simply a good friend and neighbor. He'd help out anyone who needed it.

Grace turned away from the window and focused her thoughts on tablecloths, plant and flower arrangements, and groupings of antiques that would reflect their theme of the Revolutionary War.

That reminded her of the stunning blue dress Winnie had designed for her. Grace's cheeks warmed as she pictured how Spencer would react when he saw her wearing it.

But she didn't know if he would even show up.

"Lydia?" Grace tapped lightly on the door of the Buttercup Suite.

Grace and Charlotte thought they had heard faint movement inside as they'd gone up and down the stairs, carrying decor from the hall closets on the second floor. Still, no one had emerged, and with the afternoon waning, they'd decided to check on their guest.

"I hope we didn't imagine hearing her in there," Charlotte whispered. "But what if she's sick and can't answer the door?"

Frowning, Grace knocked again. "Lydia, it's Grace and Charlotte. Are you all right?"

After the second knock, the doorknob finally turned, and Lydia opened the door a few inches. Though fully dressed—stylishly as usual—the woman's blanched face under perfect makeup made Grace want to drag her out of her cave and feed her.

"Yes?" Lydia didn't open the door any farther. "Is something wrong?"

If you're not eating, yes, something's very wrong. "We don't mean to intrude," Grace said. "But we haven't seen you since breakfast and wondered if you were ill. Or if we could help in any way."

"Thank you, but I'm fine," Lydia said, then started to close the door.

Grace moved a step closer. "We also wanted to make sure you know you're invited to our party tonight. It's a Revolutionary War theme, and Charlotte's been cooking up her specialties all day."

"Blini with sturgeon caviar. Rosemary lamb and scallop-bacon kabobs with grilled fruit." Charlotte sounded as if she were telling her love story. "And some historical sweets, like tarts filled with ice cream and topped with crocants."

"I'm not sure if I'll feel up to a party," Lydia murmured and shut the door.

Charlotte's eyes widened in disbelief.

Grace gestured toward the stairway.

As they descended, Charlotte said, "Well, I guess you can't force people to have a good time."

"No, we can't." Grace sighed. She'd so hoped Lydia would venture out of her shell. "I wish I could help—"

"You always want to help," Charlotte interrupted. "But you can't fix everyone. You just can't."

Later, in one last attempt to coax Lydia to join her on the Candlelight Journey, Grace took a small sampler plate of her sister's hors d'oeuvres up to the Buttercup Suite. But before she knocked, she heard the woman sobbing inside the room.

Charlotte was right.

Grace set the plate by the door and left.

8

Grace

"Will you stop fussing about the party?" Charlotte said, putting her hands on her hips. "Go on the Candlelight Journey, like you planned."

"I'm sorry," Grace said. "But there are just so many details—"

"There are always so many details," her sister retorted. "Details we've taken care of. Besides, Winnie said she can come over early if something happens."

Yes, Winnie always helped at their gatherings, bless her. What would they do without their sweet aunt?

Charlotte tapped her toe. "You know perfectly well I should do the last-minute cooking stuff. If you hang around here for the next three hours, you'll make me as crazy as you are."

Grace chuckled. "All right, I'll go. But call if you need me."

"I won't."

Grace shook her head, then texted Mimi Beale, her outgoing friend and the choir director at Fellowship Christian Church, who appeared at the inn's door a little later.

"I thought I'd have to drag you out of here," Mimi teased.

"You might have, if Charlotte hadn't kicked me out," Grace admitted.

They both laughed as they got into Mimi's car and headed to historic downtown Magnolia Harbor.

Grace gazed out the window and sighed. "It doesn't seem fair that I'm going on the walk the night of our party, leaving Charlotte holding the bag. When she goes tomorrow night, all the brouhaha will be over. I won't have to worry about a thing."

"She knows you need to lighten up. It's time you had some fun," Mimi advised. "Besides, wasn't this big bash her idea?"

"I guess it was."

"Of course it was," Mimi said. "If I hear even a hint of guilt from you the rest of the evening, the girls and I will toss you into the swamp."

As they parked and exited the car, Grace dispatched all thoughts of Charlotte's absence and the small, circling worry about Lydia's troubles that had threatened to settle in her stomach.

They walked to the Heritage Library on Willow Street, where the Candlelight Journey began, and met up with Judith, Helen, and Patty.

"I was just telling Judith and Helen about Billy's latest role," Patty said.

Patty often shared stories about her son, Billy, who had moved to Los Angeles and was attempting to make it as an actor. So far, he had only landed obscure and minor parts in commercials and TV shows. One of his most notable roles was a lawn care technician in an episode of *NCIS*. Billy hadn't had any lines, but he could be seen fertilizing the grass in the background.

"What was it for?" Mimi asked.

"A commercial for a restaurant," Patty replied. "Billy was one of the diners in the background. When the waiter walked over, he tripped and spilled a pitcher of ice water all over Billy."

The women laughed.

"Several groups have already left for the first segment of the walk," Judith said, glancing around. "Are we ready?"

Helen nodded. "Let's go."

Having seen the homes' interiors many times, Grace and her friends simply ambled along the cobblestone streets, inhaling the fragrance of magnolia and watching homeowners light lanterns and candles in their windows and gorgeous gardens.

Several volunteers in colonial dress lit an unbroken line of votive candles along the main street.

Grace considered it one of her favorite festival moments. Memories of walking with her family, holding Charlotte's chubby toddler hand, flooded her thoughts. When Charlotte had noticed the candles, she'd begun singing "Happy Birthday" and blowing them out. Only Winnie could talk Charlotte into letting the candles burn.

Winnie.

Grace couldn't recall the last time she'd walked this route without her aunt. Even during high school, college, and the years after she'd married Hank, Grace had managed to stroll a portion of the Candlelight Journey with Winnie. After Hank and her parents had passed, Grace and Winnie had clung to the custom and each other more than ever.

But yesterday, when she'd tried to talk Winnie into walking even a block with her, Winnie had dug in her heels. No way would she attend the festival. Period. Discussion over.

Grace missed Winnie. She wiped away a tear in the corner of her right eye.

Mimi seemed to sense Grace's mood and squeezed her shoulder.

When Helen wistfully mentioned the house both she and Winnie considered their favorite, did a shadow settle over Patty's face?

If so, Patty recovered quickly. "Okay, how many of us are older than that house?" She pointed to a French mansion built in the early 1800s. "Not me, of course."

Judith laughed. "No, you're older than the dirt in the garden."

Grace kept turning to share the banter with her aunt, only to realize she wasn't there. How she missed Winnie's teasing. She always joked that they couldn't keep up with her.

Winnie was the heart of the Candlelight Journey Festival. To celebrate it without her seemed wrong.

More tears threatened, but Grace corralled them with the reminder that Winnie would at least come to the party tonight.

"Grace!"

She turned to see who had called her name.

Ian waved and strode to her side. He was dressed in a colonial soldier's outfit, complete with a blue coat, a black tricorn hat, and gloves. His long legs were encased in blue knee breeches and white stockings. "I didn't think I would see you before the party."

Patty smiled. "Grace, why don't you introduce us to this handsome gentleman?"

Grace had to admit that Ian did cut a romantic figure. "This is Dr. Ian Southby, a historian and guest at our inn."

Her friends greeted him warmly.

Judith, bless her, nudged Patty with an elbow. Grace knew it was a hint to knock off the matchmaking.

Then Judith faced Ian. "You certainly have joined in the spirit of our festival," she said, steering the conversation to historical matters. "Please tell us about your costume."

Ian seemed only too happy to accommodate her. "This uniform is a replica of a Revolutionary War captain's, as indicated by the gold epaulet on my right shoulder, red waist sash, white ribbon cockade on my hat, and brass sword hilt.

"American soldiers didn't necessarily dress this well, of course," Ian continued. "Some of them were lucky to have shoes during cold weather." He gestured at his fake ponytail, which blended well with his own black waves. "They didn't always powder their hair either, especially when fighting in the swamps."

Then Ian offered numerous insights they hadn't heard about the town's French heritage and lifestyles during the colonial era. Fortunately, Grace's friends all enjoyed history.

Grace vacillated between enjoying his fascinating bits of information and missing their usual girlfriend fun. If only he didn't take her arm in such a courtly way, bringing a faint tingle to her own arm. If only the other women would keep their gazes on the mansions.

Soon Patty left to prepare for the play. Grace and the others lit flameless candles and followed a tour guide's lantern around an outer boundary of dark, shadowy wetlands. During the Revolutionary War, it was one of the places Francis Marion, the Swamp Fox, had outmaneuvered British troops.

By that time, Grace—and the others, she imagined—had heard enough historical details. But Ian showed no signs of winding down.

The affable, elderly tour guide gave up leading until they approached a particularly gloomy swamp. The oily waters seemed to suck the light from their candles.

"Think how creepy this place must be at midnight," Mimi whispered.

Grace didn't have to imagine. She'd gone on the extended midnight tour once when Hank had talked her into witnessing the heart-squeezing reenactment of an ambush.

Even on this peaceful night, black cypress trees surrounded the group with mossy, twisted limbs, and owl calls sounded so eerie that tourists gasped. Despite the familiarity of the landscape, Grace, her friends, and the other townspeople quieted. Even Ian paused in his treatise.

Their guide stepped forward, the lantern lighting his eye sockets and making him resemble a glowing skull. "Some say the ghost of the Swamp Fox still roams these forests, warning anyone who approaches that this land is forever his." He lowered his voice to a gravelly, menacing tone. "Are you friend or foe, you who trespass on his territory? Sometimes the Swamp Fox does not bother to find out."

There was a bloodcurdling shout.

Screams rang out all around Grace. Something clawed her arm, and she must have jumped a foot.

The guide shifted his lantern toward Ian. "Sir, are you all right?"

"Something slid over my foot," Ian choked out, clutching at Grace. "Is it a rattler?"

An older man in the group shone his candle on a tiny reptile. "Actually, it was probably this little lizard. I'm surprised you didn't scare him to death." He picked it up and wiggled it at Ian, who jumped again.

Chuckles broke out on every side.

So much for this brave captain. Grace seized the opportunity to pull away from him.

Despite the break in the spooky atmosphere, the guide managed to regain most of his listeners' attention with whimsical descriptions of nocturnal swamp animals. Darting bats added to his nature lesson.

Ian remained blessedly quiet as they walked back to the library, where the tour ended.

A block or two away, Spencer's tall, athletic figure materialized on the sidewalk. After Ian's drama, her neighbor looked especially appealing, with his conservative yet casual shirt and khakis.

Grace smiled and waved at Spencer.

His smile of recognition spread across his face like sunshine through the clouds.

Until his gaze rested on Ian.

The hand he'd raised in greeting froze halfway. Spencer's smile now held all the warmth of a blank computer screen. He turned and disappeared into the shadows.

Grace didn't remember what she said to Ian before she and Mimi told the others goodbye and headed back to the inn to prepare for the party.

But as she donned the beautiful blue dress Winnie had made, she was pretty sure Spencer would never see it.

Charlotte

"Never in my life have I seen such an incredible spread." Howard Mailer, a prominent businessman from Columbia, took a blin with caviar. He paused, eyes closed, to savor the bite-size Russian pancake with its crème fraîche and black pearly topping. "Delicious."

"I'm so glad you're enjoying our little party." Charlotte found it easy to smile. She didn't know exactly how many gatherings she had catered, but this one had to be the best she'd ever achieved—so far.

"You're certainly showing your appreciation, dear," his wife said. She smiled at Charlotte. "The food is exquisite, and I must say I'm not surprised. You wrote those marvelous cookbooks, didn't you? I do hope you have another one in the works."

Charlotte briefly told the woman about her current project.

Other visitors joined them, and as they chatted, Charlotte glanced over at Dean lingering nearby. As always, he looked great. He wore black pants and a gunmetal-gray shirt with his usual style. She stifled a grin. Dean couldn't help but hear every word of the continuous adulation for her food.

Not only had her hors d'oeuvres won rave reviews from nearly everyone, but her historical, edible art had attracted the attention of a visiting writer for a prominent culinary magazine. The woman had snapped some photos of Charlotte's creations and requested a future interview. The fragile crocants—lacy, dome-like covers over crystal dishes of various creams—had frustrated Charlotte at times, but they proved to have been worth it. The crowning touch was her gilded, sugar-dough reproduction of the inn's front doors and porch.

Listening to the praise, Charlotte had to admit that she couldn't have pulled off this amazing array of culinary delights without plenty of assistance from her sister and her aunt.

Grace, stunning in her blue gown, had handled the invitations, the RSVPs, and much of the decorating. Her sister really did possess a flair for event design, Charlotte reflected as she took in the decor once again.

Replicas of banners, letters, and antiques from the Revolutionary War era adorned the foyer. They were accented by sumptuous red-and-white bouquets and illuminated by elegant silver candelabras. Guests visited tables that would have graced the dining room of a colonial governor, and the veranda had never been more elegant. Yet somehow, with Grace's traffic flow plan and conversational groupings, she'd achieved the casual efficiency of a modern gathering.

Now Grace was doing her usual hostess magic, floating among clusters of guests, coaxing loners into groups, and making sure everyone was relaxed and happy.

Winnie was lovely in a peach gown with a golden petticoat. She cheerfully served and mingled with guests.

Joining her occasionally for banter, laughs, and hugs, Charlotte rejoiced that the party had made her aunt forget her hurt—at least for this evening. The soiree had been a great idea all around.

She waved at Bonnie, marveling at the ease with which the woman engaged strangers. If Bonnie and Grace joined forces to befriend the world, no human being would ever feel left out.

Tom, his injured hand still wrapped in a bandage, seemed to have recovered well. He alternately refilled his crystal plate at the refreshments table and tagged along after his wife.

Daniel and Maggie had made an appearance—long enough for Daniel to fill a plate twice—but they still lived and breathed in a honeymoon bubble that soon floated out the door. Charlotte watched them leave.

They were an adorable couple. Charlotte smiled as she brushed a stray crumb from the glimmering folds of her green gown that, despite her refusal to wear an apron, had stayed free of stains all evening.

Dean wandered over to Charlotte. "You and Grace really outdid yourselves this time." Genuine admiration shone in his eyes and voice.

Admiration for the party only? Dean's gaze lingered on her, and Charlotte's cheeks warmed. "Thank you. I hope you're enjoying yourself."

"Absolutely. The food and wine are great, and I've met a bunch of interesting people."

Ignoring a poke from her better judgment, she asked, "Did you taste the caviar blini?"

"Of course I did." Dean grinned. "They're excellent. But I wouldn't expect anything less from the queen of appetizers."

Charlotte smiled. Perhaps he had decided to employ his party manners tonight.

"I like a little more heat in my blini and caviar. Maybe just a touch of cayenne in the crème fraîche," Dean added. "Be sure to taste mine tomorrow night."

Her satisfaction faded, and she fought an immature retort. When Dean ended their chat and walked away, she felt her shoulders slightly relax.

Charlotte turned her attention to the other guests. As she circulated among the crowd, a few people inquired about future bookings at the inn. Two women were searching for locations for their children's weddings and wanted to tour the inn's facilities. The head of a corporation requested information about retreat possibilities, and a historian asked about renting the entire inn for meetings during next year's Candlelight Journey Festival.

When Charlotte told Grace the news, she couldn't help but give her a triumphant look. She didn't rub it in, of course. She didn't have to. Grace was probably adding up all the dollars and cents in her head already.

A tiny catch in her sister's smile made Charlotte turn. It was Ian again. How long had he been hovering around Grace like that?

Pushing her gloat aside, Charlotte steered Ian away from Grace and over to the foyer's display of copies of historical letters and documents. Only truly interested guests lingered there. Exuding charm that would have made her sister proud, Charlotte captured a few such guests and handed them over to Ian, and they made each other happy for more than fifteen minutes. Long enough for Grace to catch her breath.

She whispered her thanks to Charlotte and appeared to enjoy her freedom, but Charlotte still detected an odd restlessness in her sister. Grace usually focused on her guests to the point of ignoring burning smells from the oven. But tonight, she scanned the room as if expecting someone any minute. Was she still obsessing about Lydia? Hoping that against all odds, their unhappy guest would show up?

Charlotte also found it odd that when the last delighted guest finally departed—including Ian, who went out for coffee with a few other history buffs—Grace didn't change into jeans. The dresses Winnie had made for them were gorgeous but awkward to move around in. She and Charlotte still had to put away leftovers and clear up the worst of the mess.

A knock on the back door solved the mystery.

Spencer. Dressed in a T-shirt and jeans.

Charlotte smothered a gasp. She'd totally forgotten he'd been invited to the party.

Grace, composed as ever, assumed her hostess smile. But blue sparks glinted, then smoldered in her eyes.

Charlotte waited for Spencer to apologize or at least explain his absence.

But Spencer merely said, "Where do you want me to start?"

Grace pointed to the foyer. "I've taken down the antique displays. Please fold up the tables there. I'll be back in a moment." She strode to her suite, the elegant dress flowing behind her.

Charlotte choked back a laugh. Sometime during the past week, Grace and Spencer had set each other off. The teardown tonight might prove far more interesting than Charlotte had expected.

Not that the tiff slowed their progress. Grace's efficiency always kicked into overdrive when she was mad, and Spencer moved and carried like a well-programmed robot.

Charlotte had to hustle to keep up with them. It wasn't fair. She just wanted to sit down with a glass of iced tea and watch the fireworks.

At least they were on track to finish in record time. Charlotte was glad because she would have to get up early to cook breakfast for the guests. Even if some of them slept in and skipped the meal, Ian seemed to hit the floor running every morning, no matter how late he stayed out.

As she loaded the dishwasher and washed fragile crystal and china, Charlotte consoled herself with fond—and sometimes smug—remembrances of the night's success. The tours of the inn for the two mothers. The interview with the magazine writer. The retreats and meetings their open house might very well generate, not only this year but for years to come.

Soaking in a warm pool of self-congratulation, she was able to brush away Dean's critique of her food.

Something chilled her thoughts, though. Something small, like a single, large raindrop on a sunny day. What was it?

Other raindrops fell occasionally as she washed the kitchen counters and gave the floor a quick mop.

Had she said something? Done something? Burned the bacon on a kabob?

When she couldn't think of anything, Charlotte pushed the annoying thoughts aside.

"If there's nothing else, I'll be going," Spencer said.

"No, that's it," Grace said. "Thanks for all your help." Her tone was chilly.

Charlotte echoed her sister's gratitude, but she doubted Spencer heard it before he tramped out the door.

As they put away clean dishes, Charlotte couldn't help but take the opportunity to tease her sister, who was always so composed. "My goodness, Spencer can work like a mule."

A pause. "Yes, he certainly can." Grace tossed good silverware into the drawer as if it were plastic.

Despite her energetic cleanup, Grace sounded tired. Charlotte realized it wasn't the best time to kid her sister about their neighbor.

When they finished tidying the kitchen, Charlotte had cooled down about their other neighbor. Why had she let Dean's comments about her food get to her even a little bit? After such an exhausting day, she wanted to sleep for a few hours before breakfast prep, not toss and turn because of his remarks.

She and Grace shared a hug before Charlotte left for her cottage.

Sometimes her comfortable bed felt almost as good as a gourmet meal tasted.

Almost.

Still needing to wind down, she indulged in remembering how many visitors had complimented the food and the inn.

But amid her drowsy euphoria, the raindrop annoyance reemerged. Charlotte buried her head in her pillow, but its drip, drip, drip on her thoughts refused to go away.

What was still bothering her? She really had dismissed Dean as not worth fussing about. And she and Grace had already made up after their argument over the party.

Memories of her mother's insisting they say, "I forgive you," as children made Charlotte both shake her head and smile. No wonder her mother had loved that Bible verse that was written on the sampler.

The sampler.

Charlotte sat bolt upright.

Had she imagined the wall where it had hung was now bare?

Grace

"I can't believe someone stole the sampler," Charlotte said.

Grace stared at the empty spot on the hallway wall, speechless.

Winston, at her knee, cocked his head. He gazed at the wall too, as if it would help him comprehend his humans' distress.

The dog had seemed to understand when Grace and Charlotte wanted him to remain in Grace's private quarters in case any of the party guests suffered from animal allergies. If Winston had sensed something amiss, he would have run to her or Charlotte and whined. Apparently, the robber hadn't raised any red flags as far as Winston was concerned.

So had the thief attended their party?

Grace pressed her hands against her temples. Not only had every smiling guest at their open house become a suspect, but saying goodbye to the sampler seemed like yet another miniature goodbye to her mother.

The faint fragrance of Charlotte's perfume encircled them as she enveloped Grace in a fierce hug.

For a silent moment, they stood together, empty as the sampler's spot on the wall.

Concern for their household tugged Grace's thoughts back to the present. "We have to make sure everyone's safe."

Charlotte frowned. "Right, but shouldn't we let the police do that?"

Grace visualized a scenario with sirens, officers, and interrogations during the wee hours of the morning. "That'll scare our guests to death.

The whole bunch might pack up and leave. Besides, whoever did this might have already left hours ago."

Before she lost her nerve, Grace grabbed her master key and a flashlight from a kitchen drawer. Hurrying to the living room, Winston at her heels, she took a poker from the fireplace. "I'll go upstairs first." She pointed at Charlotte. "Follow me and keep your phone ready to call 911."

Charlotte shook her head, but she tiptoed up the dimly lit steps behind her sister.

Grace smothered a sudden, bizarre giggle. They must look like heroines in a mystery movie from the 1940s.

"What's the matter with you?" Charlotte whispered. "You're supposed to be the sensible one."

Grace didn't bother to explain how this night had carried away logic like sticks in a stream. Instead, she aimed the flashlight around the landing and the hallway. No burglar. Bouquets and candlesticks were in place, with nothing missing. Realizing she hadn't exhaled lately, Grace let out a sigh of relief. So far, so good.

Charlotte joined Grace as she halted outside the Bluebell Suite.

Grace raised a hand and mouthed, "Listen."

Snoring, loud and rhythmic as a percussion section, issued from the room.

Apparently, Tom hadn't been disturbed in the least. And if Tom had spent a serene night, the odds were that Bonnie, staying in the Rosebud Suite, had too.

They heard Lydia stirring in the Buttercup Suite, but her steps didn't sound agitated. More likely, Grace thought, she was sleeping about as much as she was eating. Surely Lydia would have called if she'd encountered trouble.

During the party cleanup, Grace had not seen Daniel, Maggie, or

Ian go to their rooms. Could they have returned, evading Grace's notice?

Charlotte rolled her eyes, so Grace knew that she was also considering the possible embarrassment of lingering outside the honeymooners' room. But a running faucet in the Dogwood Suite bathroom released them from that risk.

Grace could not face checking the Wisteria Loft Suite. What if Ian had indeed returned and now caught her outside his door? She pressed the key and flashlight into Charlotte's hand and told her to take Winston up to the third floor.

Charlotte complied, but her reluctance was evident.

While Grace waited on the stairs, holding her phone, she recalled Ian's obsession with the missing sampler. She pushed the possibility away, hating even the suggestion that a guest might have robbed them.

Besides, the historian, though quirky, wasn't stupid. If he'd planned to steal the sampler, surely he wouldn't have made his fascination with it so obvious. Still, when she refused his offer, perhaps his determination to own it had overcome his better judgment. Had he acted impulsively?

Charlotte and Winston soon returned.

"What happened?" Grace whispered.

"I didn't hear a thing, so I knocked," Charlotte explained in a low voice. "Not sure what I would have said if he'd answered, but fortunately, he didn't. I opened the room, but there was no sign of him, and everything looked undisturbed. He must still be out with his friends." She scratched behind the dog's ears. "Winston seemed fine, so I think we're all clear."

"We're clear upstairs anyway. We'd better check out the main floor more thoroughly."

The three of them descended the stairs. After flooding the downstairs with light, they searched the rooms but found no evidence the doors had been forced open or that anything else was missing. They paused in the foyer.

"This is crazy," Grace said. "Why would someone risk arrest for one sampler? You'd think the Bible verse on it would have dissuaded whoever it was."

"Unless he stole from the barn or shed too." Charlotte frowned. "You don't want to check outside, do you?"

Grace cringed at the thought of trekking through the steamy, shadowy night. "No way. We'll let the police do that."

Besides, would a thief who'd presumably taken only a religious needlework sampler from the house steal from the shed too? Her foggy brain pictured Ian in colonial dress, sampler under his arm, riding off into the night on their lawn mower.

"Maybe the sampler will somehow turn up by morning," Charlotte suggested. "Ian might have borrowed it to show his friends."

"Right," Grace said, but she was sure Charlotte didn't believe it either.

Charlotte yawned. "I'm dying for some rest."

Grace glanced at the grandfather clock. It was late, and her weary body begged for sleep. "Me too. If the police came right now, I don't think I could make sense if I tried."

But would she and her sister sleep? Even if she summoned enough courage to walk Charlotte to the cottage, Grace couldn't tolerate the thought of leaving her sister there alone. She didn't like the idea of walking back to the inn and being isolated in her apartment either.

"Want to stay with me tonight?" Grace asked, trying to sound casual.

Charlotte smiled. "I thought you'd never ask."

Once they were settled in bed, Grace wondered if she'd ever fall asleep. She'd forgotten her sister's habit of inching her cold toes up Grace's calf.

A few hours later, her alarm's uncouth buzz roused her from ocean-deep slumber. She sat up.

Charlotte didn't stir.

Winston, who usually sprang into action well before the alarm rang, now glared at the clock as if it were a chattering squirrel on a tree's top branch.

She shut off the alarm and poked Charlotte. "Wake up. We have to call the police. Putting it off isn't going to make this go away."

"Did you move the sampler?" Ian asked as he entered the dining room. After being out so late last night, he was still up early this morning. "You did not sell it to someone else, did you?"

"No, I did not move it or sell it," Grace replied. "It appears to have been stolen."

His jaw dropped. "How horrible. What a dishonorable, despicable, dastardly thing to do!"

Grace nodded. "The police will soon arrive to handle it."

Ian finally awakened to the possible insult he'd dealt her. "I am sorry I questioned your integrity and overlooked your safety and that of your sister. I am as culpable as that scoundrel. Forgive me, dear lady." He took her hand and kissed it. "I spoke before I thought."

He continued talking as Charlotte served him her elegant seafood frittata. The other guests hadn't arrived for breakfast yet.

When Grace attempted to take refuge in the kitchen, Ian followed her and pulled up a stool to the island, censuring the thief while he devoured his breakfast.

Are you talking about yourself? Grace thought, but she still couldn't believe that he was involved in the theft. Whatever his faults, the man seemed incapable of pretense.

Unless his entire persona was built on some bizarre attempt to disguise his true identity.

The bell above the front door jingled.

Grace and Charlotte rushed to the foyer. Ian trailed them.

Winston beat them all there and greeted Lieutenant Wesley Townsend, who stood at the front desk. The man leaned down and patted the dog.

"Thank you for coming so early," Grace said, resisting the urge to hug the big man.

"Glad to help." He straightened, then raised his eyebrows slightly as he glanced over her shoulder at Ian.

Now accustomed to Ian, Grace realized how the man's usual theatrical attire might startle the officer. She introduced her guest, who released a barrage of entreaty.

"That sampler is a marvelous example of the textile art of the colonial period," Ian told the lieutenant. "You simply must find it." He proceeded to rattle off historical information, including a list of young ladies' finishing schools and their needlecraft teachers from the late eighteenth century.

The information assault seemed to stun Townsend. But only for a moment. "Sir, I appreciate your knowledge about the stolen item, and we'll talk about it soon, so please don't leave the inn. First, I'll examine the premises and speak with these ladies." He gestured toward Grace and Charlotte. "Alone, please."

Ian drew himself up as if offended, but he headed toward the back veranda.

The lieutenant asked Grace and Charlotte to accompany him to the hallway, where he dusted for fingerprints.

Townsend frowned at the results. "There are a few partial prints, but nothing is very clear. After we check them at the station, I'll let you know if anything solid turns up."

"Thank you," Grace said.

He noted the downstairs entrances and exits. "Were all the doors unlocked last night?"

"We leave the doors open during the day, but only the front doors were unlocked during the party," Grace answered.

When Townsend returned from examining the barn, the shed, and Charlotte's cottage, he confirmed they showed no signs of entry. "Is there a private place where we can discuss the theft in more detail?"

Grace motioned to the living room. "Would you care for coffee this morning? Maybe one of Charlotte's pastries?"

The man's official veneer melted into a grin. "Sounds great."

As Grace ushered Townsend to a chair in the living room, Charlotte disappeared into the kitchen. A few moments later, she handed the lieutenant a cup of coffee and a cherry turnover, then sat down on the sofa next to her sister.

"Thank you," Townsend said. He removed a notepad and a pen from his pocket. "Now let's get down to business."

In no time, he'd questioned both Grace and Charlotte about their search of the inn. He recorded all the names of the inn's guests, their background information, and their whereabouts, as far as Grace and Charlotte knew, the past several days.

Grace didn't want to accuse Ian, but she told the lieutenant about the historian's offer to buy the sampler and her refusal. "It holds a lot of sentimental value for my sister and me. Our mother reminded us of that Bible verse every time we quarreled as children."

"Sounds like my mom," Townsend said with a chuckle.

His laughter lifted Grace's melancholy for a moment.

Then the lieutenant turned serious as he asked Grace to bring in Ian and the other guests as they came downstairs.

"Of course." Grace hurried out of the room. She found Ian reading a book on the veranda. "Excuse me. Lieutenant Townsend is in the living room, and he'd like to ask you a few questions."

"I suppose he believes I'm the main suspect in this business," Ian replied, setting the book aside.

Grace tried not to wince. "He hasn't said that."

Ian snorted. "He does not have to. He accused me the moment he laid eyes on me."

"Lieutenant Townsend has a reputation for being thorough and fair," Grace said. "I'm sure he'll hear you out."

"I have nothing to hide." With a dramatic gesture, Ian brushed back a lock of hair and marched to the living room.

Grace and Charlotte joined forces to tidy up the remaining mess from the party before the other guests came downstairs. They didn't intend to eavesdrop on Lieutenant Townsend's interrogation.

But Ian spoke loudly, making sure everyone within earshot knew he had nothing to hide and was innocent of any wrongdoing. He'd last seen the sampler when he'd helped himself to a bottle of water from the refrigerator. It was right before he'd left for the festival the previous evening.

"Did you attend the party here last night?" Townsend asked.

"Yes," Ian said.

Grace and Charlotte could have vouched for him, but neither could have monitored his actions every minute. Ian could have slipped into the hallway and taken or hidden the sampler. But how could he have remained incognito while wearing that striking colonial costume?

Unless he'd lied about when he last saw the sampler. Had Ian stolen it before dressing for the festival? She and Charlotte had been too busy to notice much throughout the day.

"I understand you've taken a lot of interest in this sampler," Townsend said.

Grace couldn't see the lieutenant's friendly eyes turn steely, but she heard iron in his voice.

"I certainly have," Ian answered. "As I said, it's an excellent example of the era's—"

"How excellent?" Townsend interrupted. "I'll bet you can tell me how much it would fetch from a museum."

A long pause. "Well, yes. It's a particularly rare example in mint condition, so it's worth about $50,000."

Grace, sweeping the foyer, clapped a hand over her mouth.

Charlotte's eyes bugged out.

"I also understand you offered Ms. Porter $1,000 for it," the lieutenant continued.

"That was my first offer," Ian clarified. "My second offer was more."

There was silence for a few moments. Then Ian burst out, "You can't arrest me for wanting a bargain."

Townsend didn't respond to the remark. Instead, he said, "We would appreciate it if you remain in the area."

"I will stay as long as necessary and cooperate in any way I can," Ian said, stiffening his tone. "But as I stated before, I have nothing to hide. About a hundred people attended the party last night. Any one of them could have been aware of the sampler's value and stolen it. After a thorough and objective investigation, you will find that I am not responsible."

An exit sentence. Grace rushed to the kitchen, Charlotte on her heels, lest Townsend think they'd been listening at the door. As they peeked from the kitchen door, both caught a glimpse of Ian sailing from the room, head thrown back in righteous wrath.

Or not so righteous. Grace had believed the historian incapable of pretense. But given the sampler's $50,000 price tag, perhaps he was a better actor than she had thought.

11

Grace

Grace and Charlotte had sampled exactly two bites of seafood frittata apiece when Tom and Bonnie appeared in the dining room, eyes wide.

"Why the police car?" Bonnie asked, glancing from Grace to Charlotte. "Is something wrong? Are you two all right?"

"We're okay," Grace assured her, then explained about the missing sampler.

Bonnie put her hand over her heart. "Goodness gracious."

"That's terrible," Tom added.

"We're just thankful no one appears to have confronted the thief," Grace said as she patted Bonnie's arm.

"We have an excellent police department in Magnolia Harbor," Charlotte chimed in. "They'll do everything possible to keep us safe."

"This is such a lovely inn." Now Bonnie patted Grace's shoulder. "We're so sorry this happened to you."

"I'm sure the police will help us recover the sampler." Grace summoned an apologetic smile. "I'm sorry, but the lieutenant will want to talk to everyone in the house, including you."

Tom nodded. "Anything we can do to help."

"Right now, it's also important to find out if the thief stole from anyone else," Grace continued. "Would you like to eat breakfast? Or would you prefer to search your belongings first?"

Tom gazed at the frittata and pastries. "We've locked our doors even when just coming downstairs, so I can't imagine anybody could get into our rooms."

Following his cue, Bonnie said, "A bite to eat and your fabulous coffee does sound wonderful."

Serving the couple seemed so nice and normal. Upon discovering the sisters had eaten little, Bonnie insisted they sit down too. As if they were the hosts, she and Tom told charming stories of their South American travels.

The couple's obvious efforts to distract them didn't make Grace forget their problems, but it was pleasant to sit in the morning sunshine and converse as if nothing bad had happened.

Only toward the meal's end did Bonnie's curiosity emerge. "Was the missing sampler the one Ian showed us in the kitchen hallway?"

Grace, not wanting to incriminate the man, tried to keep her tone light. "Yes, I believe he covered that—along with the rest of the planet's history—during hospitality hour."

Bonnie's sharp eyes met Grace's, but she said nothing more.

They were all drinking their second cup of coffee when Townsend appeared.

After Grace made the introductions, the lieutenant asked Tom and Bonnie to search their suites, then join him in the living room.

"Of course." Tom ushered his wife upstairs.

"I'll wait for them," Townsend said and went to stand by the bottom of the stairs.

When Grace and Charlotte were alone, they took the plates to the kitchen and started cleaning up.

"Are you going to talk to Lydia?" Charlotte asked.

For the past half hour, Grace had been ignoring the thought. Yet why should she handle all the sticky situations? "Perhaps you could? You two clicked during hospitality hour."

"Sure, when we were talking about wine and cheese." Charlotte shook her head. "You're the expert when it comes to dealing with hurting people."

Grace had to admit that Charlotte was right. Lydia needed to be handled with care. "Okay, I'll go." Taking a pastry on a plate, Grace headed upstairs.

Not to her surprise, the woman had dressed with her usual flair. However, her calm reception of the bad news took Grace aback.

A tiny, mirthless smile tugged at Lydia's mouth. "I live in New York. Theft is an everyday occurrence."

"I'm sorry, but the police will want to talk to you and everyone else staying here," Grace said.

"I'll be glad to talk to them," Lydia answered. "But I don't think I'll be able to supply any useful information. I was gone most of yesterday, you know."

Actually, I didn't know. The woman came and went like a shadow. Grace persuaded her to accept the pastry, but she doubted Lydia would eat it. "There's a party at The Tidewater this evening, and you're more than welcome to attend. Charlotte and I will be going, and I believe the other guests will be there too."

"I'm not sure if I'll make it," Lydia admitted.

"Well, I hope to see you there," Grace said before she retreated.

Later Grace took tea out to Tom and Bonnie, who were knitting on the veranda.

"When we searched our rooms, we didn't find anything missing," Tom announced.

"I'm so glad to hear that," Grace said.

"Our interview with the lieutenant seemed so ordinary, like we were discussing the weather," Tom went on.

"We told him that Ian had lectured us about the sampler during hospitality hour," Bonnie said. "But he'd discussed at least twenty historical topics since we met him, so I didn't attach any importance to it."

Tom nodded. "I mostly remember talking about travel destinations with Spencer and Dean that night."

"Do you remember if Ian attended the party here last night?" Grace asked.

They both shook their heads.

"After we were done," Bonnie said, "the lieutenant asked me to fetch Lydia."

Tom shook a finger at his wife. "But he didn't ask you to eavesdrop on her interview."

"Can I help it if I'm interested in people?" Bonnie retorted, eyes twinkling. "Her interview wasn't wildly exciting. She said she'd found Ian's sampler lecture provocative, though she herself dealt mostly with contemporary textiles. She'd spent the day and evening of the theft in neighboring small towns, trying to avoid the festival."

Daniel and Maggie strolled onto the veranda.

"Good morning," Grace said.

"Sorry we missed breakfast," Maggie said.

"No need to apologize," Grace answered. "There's still food in the kitchen if you're hungry."

Daniel grinned. "I sure am."

"Why don't you two have a seat while I get your plates?" Grace went to the kitchen. She heated up some frittatas and slid several pastries onto a platter.

Charlotte entered the room. "What's going on?"

"Daniel and Maggie are hungry, so I'm taking some food out to them."

"Let me help." Charlotte retrieved orange juice from the fridge, then helped Grace carry the plates and drinks to the veranda.

When Grace set a plate in front of Daniel, he immediately dug in. "Thanks," he said around a mouthful of frittata.

Maggie turned to Grace and Charlotte with a frown. "Tom and Bonnie just told us about the theft. That's terrible."

"I'm sure the police will get to the bottom of it," Charlotte said.

"Do you remember anything about the sampler?" Grace asked. "It was hanging in the kitchen hallway."

"No, I don't recall seeing it," Maggie answered. She turned to her husband. "Do you?"

Daniel polished off the frittata, then wiped his mouth with a napkin. "No, I didn't see it either."

Townsend walked onto the veranda and addressed Daniel and Maggie. "When you're finished with breakfast, I'd like to ask the two of you a few questions."

"No problem," Daniel said.

"In the meantime, could you give me the party guest list?" the lieutenant asked Grace and Charlotte.

Grace couldn't help thinking his job would have proven far easier if her sister hadn't gotten her way. With twenty guests—versus a hundred—the odds of finding the culprit would have been much better.

Charlotte carefully avoided Grace's eyes as she e-mailed the list to Townsend. "Will you have to talk directly with all of them?"

"Not necessarily." He smiled, as if to reassure her. "I hope we can track this guy down quickly so we won't have to."

Grace didn't think Ian was a criminal. She didn't *want* to think Ian was a criminal. But his guilt certainly would prevent the phone calls her less-than-optimistic imagination now dramatized. "Hello, this is the police. Did you steal a sampler from the Magnolia Harbor Inn?"

Phone calls to a hundred potential guests.

Glancing at Charlotte's downcast face, Grace knew she was thinking the same thing.

After an exhausting night and day, neither Grace nor Charlotte felt like going to the festival, but they went to Dean's party at The Tidewater, as planned.

"Why does he always try to outdo us?" Charlotte whispered as she and Grace entered his restaurant.

Grace smoothed her violet silk dress. "It's not a competition," she whispered back. Their tastes were different from Dean's. Why compare apples with oranges?

But Grace had to admit that a small pang of envy niggled at her. The Tidewater was even more stunning than usual. Eye-catching collections of clocks and bottles, both modern and antique, struck the perfect balance with the minimalist decor. A talented musician played mellow jazz on a shiny baby grand piano near a large window that captured the full moon's rays.

Dean, who had blended similar neutrals in a trendy blazer, shirt, and pants, greeted Grace and Charlotte. "Glad you could come tonight. I was so sorry to hear about your trouble."

Of course he'd heard about the theft. The Magnolia Harbor grapevine never failed.

"Thank you," Grace said. "We're confident the police will find who took our sampler in no time."

"I'm sure they will. But don't think about that tonight." He sent a surprisingly gentle look Charlotte's way. "Come have something to eat and unwind. You definitely deserve it."

She watched Charlotte's shoulders, tense in the fluttery blue top, relax. Maybe Dean's thoughtfulness would disperse any comments her sister might make about superegos.

At times, the man could be so charming. Grace hoped his pleasant demeanor would last. They could use a quiet evening.

Dean led them to the refreshments table. Black and pewter trays of colorful appetizers made Grace's mouth water.

Despite a bartender's presence, Dean poured their choices of wine into oddly shaped, but somehow elegant, crystal glasses. He handed them their wine, then motioned to the food. "Please help yourselves."

Grace almost wished they didn't have to eat, partly because she'd stuffed herself with Charlotte's goodies the night before. Mostly, though, she dreaded Charlotte's inevitable comparison of Dean's offerings to her own.

Her sister would demand Grace's opinion of his hors d'oeuvres— especially Dean's caviar blini with the cayenne that he'd bragged about.

Steeling herself, Grace chose a few roasted veggies, fresh berries with cream, and the caviar blin.

As she'd expected, Charlotte was already nibbling one red-sprinkled blin.

Dean watched, obviously awaiting her verdict.

Maybe Grace could head this conflict off at the pass. She popped the blin into her mouth. Her taste buds made an immediate ruling: the pepper's kick distracted from the caviar rather than enhanced it. "Dean, this is—"

"Certainly innovative," Charlotte interrupted.

Mouth aflame, Grace stared at her sister. She couldn't believe that Charlotte had decided to play nice.

Dean beamed. "I thought you'd appreciate the unique flavor. I'm trying to be more adventurous in my dishes."

"I've never tasted anything like it," Charlotte remarked, then took a large sip of wine.

Grace couldn't have said it better herself.

Still in shock, Grace followed Charlotte and Dean to a larger area lit mostly by strings of tiny white lights and flickering candle groupings. They greeted other guests, seated on sleek, modern sofas and chairs gathered in intimate conversation areas.

"Well, here are my girls," Winnie called out. "I was hoping you'd come tonight." She looked sophisticated in a wine-colored sheath, with her hair in a French twist.

"We wouldn't miss it," Charlotte said.

Winnie hugged Grace and Charlotte, then insisted they sit beside her and Gus.

Other guests, including Tom and Bonnie, joined them.

Lydia probably would have liked this soiree. Grace sighed, wishing she could have persuaded the reclusive woman to attend the party.

Thank heaven some people hadn't come—people like Patty and Jillian. She tried not to picture Winnie's fireworks if they had.

Grace found herself occasionally scanning the room for Spencer's tall figure. Maybe he'd arrived earlier and already left. Or perhaps he might come later—

Grace forced herself to stop. She shifted her gaze back to their lively circle, then stood to greet Daniel and Maggie.

The couple seemed to enjoy touching base with the group from the inn but soon gravitated to a cluster of twentysomethings that included new friends they'd met at the festival.

Good for them. Grace liked the smiles on their faces as they talked. Young people needed their peers. And happy guests usually begat more happy guests.

Dean introduced Jennifer Parker, an economist from Washington, D.C., and her husband, Chris, a congressional aide, to their group.

When Jennifer met Tom and Bonnie, she asked, "Have I met you before in Richmond, Virginia? It was at a bed-and-breakfast."

"No, we haven't visited Richmond—yet." Bonnie flashed her infectious smile. "We old people all look alike, you know. Same habits and everything."

Tom pointed his bandaged hand at his wife. "Speak for yourself. I plan to party tonight."

"Maybe even until eight thirty, right?" Bonnie teased.

Winnie also made the Parkers feel at home, so they stuck around. As they shared fascinating stories about Washington, a good-looking guy in his thirties wandered over to the group and struck up a conversation with Charlotte.

Within minutes, Dean appeared at Charlotte's elbow.

What a coincidence. Grinning inwardly, Grace saw Dean was handling the tête-á-tête as a host should. He really was a nice guy.

Dean couldn't have known how much Charlotte, their guests, and Grace would need a party. She appreciated the courteous invitation he'd extended to everyone at their inn.

Grace settled against Winnie's arm across the sofa's back. How nice to simply relax. Her muscles, drawn tight as a new clothesline, finally loosened.

But the next guest appearance restrung her entire body.

Ian strode into the room, a blue satin cape rippling from his shoulders. Though he wore his usual beret rather than a crown, he held his head high as if he were royalty.

How could she have possibly forgotten about him?

Grace's heart dropped when she noticed how everyone craned their necks to look at Ian. Would the rest of the evening spin like a tornado around the suspected thief?

Dean, a plastic smile glued to his face, hurried to intercept Ian and usher him toward the serving tables.

Grace's usual helping instinct vanished. Instead, she murmured to

Charlotte something about freshening up, and together they slipped from group to group toward the restroom.

Would she make it to her refuge before Ian spotted her?

Grace zipped through the restroom door and leaned against the wall, almost panting. "You didn't have to come with me."

"I had to cool down for a second." Charlotte reapplied her lipstick. "I can't believe Ian had the nerve to show his face here."

Grace couldn't either, but after all, he'd been invited. Plus, no evidence had been found to incriminate the man. "We have to remember that he's innocent until proven guilty."

Her sister rolled her eyes. "Do you have to be so fair and upstanding all the time?"

"Yes," Grace said firmly. "Especially when a situation involves our guest."

"Even if you think he did it?" Charlotte asked, turning to Grace.

She didn't respond, concentrating instead on touching up her mascara.

"So what are you going to do now?" Charlotte challenged her. "Hide in the bathroom for the rest of the evening?"

"No. I'll stay put for a few minutes while I check my e-mail." *And maybe watch a few doggy videos while Winston's not around.* Their pet hadn't taken kindly to the video of adorable Maltese puppies that she'd watched yesterday.

Charlotte smoothed a wrinkle from her top. "This is ridiculous. I'm not about to let Ian ruin the first fun evening I've had in ages." Her heels tapped the tile floor as she marched out the door.

Part of Grace cheered Charlotte's moxie, and she wondered why she couldn't be more like her sister. But then, the historian hadn't been following Charlotte around like a stray puppy.

Giving in to puppy thoughts, she watched an adorable video of beagles on her phone. Then she squared her shoulders and left the restroom, steeling herself for Ian's approach. Maybe by now, Winnie, with her instinct to defend the underdog, had drawn him into their conversation area.

As she walked into the big room, Grace saw no such scenario. Winnie bantered with their group, apparently ignoring the man she regarded as the source of her nieces' troubles. Charlotte's magnetism had once again attracted the handsome guy she'd been talking to earlier. Dean schmoozed with businessmen on the far side of the room.

Ian stood by himself near the clock display.

The elaborate outfit and his slumped shoulders spotlighted his aloneness. With a set jaw, he raised his head. Only to stare again at the floor.

No. No. Grace fought her helper instinct, but she still found herself walking toward him. What would she say? *Steal anything else lately?* She shook her head, reminding herself that he was innocent until proven guilty.

Grace walked up to Ian and smiled. "How did the rest of the Candlelight Journey Festival go?"

He turned to her, his face brightening. "Given my captain's uniform, one of the reenactors conscripted me into tonight's midnight attack."

"That's great," Grace replied. Apparently, the reenactor hadn't heard about Ian's lizard episode.

As he launched into his usual historical analysis of the battle, Grace silently prayed all reptiles—especially the rare alligator—would avoid the battle site tonight.

Ian surprised her by cutting his lecture short. "Thank you for talking to me."

The room heated ten degrees. "I appreciate your incredible store of knowledge."

"Some things exceed even the importance of history. Like courtesy." He looked her straight in the eye. "And friendship."

Grace gulped.

Ian took her hand in his gloved one and kissed it. "Good night, lovely lady." He turned, head high once more, and headed toward Dean.

How did the man manage to cut such a courageous figure?

Dean again gave an artificial smile as Ian thanked him for the evening.

Grace hoped against hope that the spotlight she'd sensed would depart with Ian. But she knew better. Even though the well-mannered locals wouldn't mention the sampler theft, their thoughts wafted through her like a palpable gust of cold wind.

Her own feelings had spun her out again too, due to the open gaze Ian had fixed on her and the warmth of his lips on her hand.

Grace sighed. Would she don a mask the rest of the evening? The effort hardly seemed worth it. Maybe Charlotte could get a ride home with Winnie and Gus.

Grace walked back toward her smiling, animated sister.

She almost missed the light touch on her arm.

Spencer.

When had he come in?

"Sorry. I didn't mean to startle you," he said. "And sorry to hear about the theft. It's not what you needed, especially on a busy weekend."

One more mention of the missing sampler should have sent her straight out the door. Instead, the compassion in his voice made her want to stay. "Thanks. It has been difficult."

"I'll bet," Spencer said. "Our police department is great, but if you'd like a little extra help, I know some people." He was retired, but he still had connections in the FBI.

"I would appreciate that so much," Grace said. Perhaps Spencer's expertise would shorten this nightmare.

"No problem," he replied. "Can I get you something to drink?"

"I wouldn't mind a glass of wine."

Spencer nodded and waved her toward Winnie's group again while he got her a drink.

For the next hour, Grace had a good time talking to Spencer and the others. Spencer seemed to sense Grace's underlying weariness, though, and offered to take her home.

Charlotte, who wanted to stay longer, waved at them as they left.

Spencer didn't say much as he drove, but that suited Grace perfectly. Tonight his silence was a comfortable place where her mind could rest.

When they arrived at the inn, Spencer entered with her. "I want to make sure things are okay. I'll poke around outside too, so don't be surprised if you hear me."

What more could she ask? Grace accepted his help with fervent thanks, then spent a few minutes cuddling with Winston before falling into bed.

When her cell phone hauled her from a deep slumber, Grace wanted to throw it out the window.

Instead, she checked the caller ID.

Charlotte? But Grace had left her the car.

Still half-asleep, she griped, "I hope you're not making these late-night calls a habit."

"It's not like I wanted to call," Charlotte retorted, "but I thought you needed to know."

"Know what?"

"Somebody stole a miniature antique clock from Dean's collection tonight."

12

Charlotte

Police Captain Keith Daley arrived at the inn early the next morning. With the second theft, he didn't bother secluding Ian while he questioned him in the dining room, where Charlotte was preparing the table for breakfast.

Charlotte and Grace alternated going to church on Sunday mornings so one of them could stay at the inn, and today was Grace's turn to attend the service.

Grace walked inside and stopped short when she saw the captain. She greeted him and Ian, then went over to Charlotte. "Why is Daley here?" she whispered.

"Maybe he's trying to warn us about Ian," Charlotte whispered back.

Grace frowned. "Just wanted to let you know that I'm heading to church."

"See you later," Charlotte said.

When Grace left, the captain took a notepad and a pen out of his pocket and turned to Ian. "Did you go to the party at The Tidewater last night?"

"Yes, I briefly attended," Ian answered. "I was invited."

"While you were there, did you notice a miniature antique clock among those on display?"

Their guest nodded. "But I had nothing to do with its theft. Anyone at the party could have pocketed it."

Charlotte barely restrained a sniff. *I'll bet he knows exactly how much that clock is worth.*

As if reading her mind, Captain Daley probed, "As a historian and antique authority, you're probably aware of the clock's value."

"Of course." For a moment, Ian defaulted to his lecture tone. "It is a French miniature from the late 1800s in excellent condition, the best I saw in that display. I would estimate its value between $5,000 and $6,000."

Charlotte was certain Ian had stolen the clock, just like he'd stolen their sampler. Surely, the police would soon find evidence against him.

But Charlotte's conscience insisted that her certainty of the historian's guilt was rooted in frustration. Ian had already destroyed the afterglow of their successful open house. Now, just when she and Brandon—the guy she'd met at The Tidewater—were getting better acquainted, their conversation had been abruptly ended by the clock's theft. During their hurried goodbye, Brandon had said he'd call her, but she didn't know if he really would.

Daley asked Ian a few more questions, then closed his notepad. "Thank you for your time. I'll be in touch if I have any further questions." He nodded at Charlotte and walked out.

After the captain's departure, Charlotte couldn't help feeling a little sorry for Ian. Lines were etched into his face, wrinkles she hadn't seen before. He trudged to the stairs and slowly climbed them to his suite—nothing like his usual vigorous pace.

Even so, Charlotte still wished there was a way to get him to leave. But she knew her sister would never throw him out, no matter what new disasters he invited to their doorstep.

Trying not to imagine any other catastrophes, Charlotte took refuge in her kitchen.

If only Ian wasn't so obnoxious. If only he would go home. If only he had chosen Mongolia instead of Magnolia Harbor as his vacation destination.

Back in top form at breakfast, Ian stood at one end of the dining room table, holding forth to the guests at the other end.

Once upon a time, breakfast around here was enjoyable. Charlotte, serving peach praline crepes, stopped gritting her teeth and pasted on a fake smile.

"Freedom from oppression has always comprised the bedrock of this country," Ian declared in an orator's voice. "Our forefathers—including Francis Marion—fought, and some offered their very lives so we would not live in fear of false accusations or the shadow of tyranny. In the same spirit, I shall not quail in the face of harassment. I shall not run away."

The speech might have proved more effective if he'd been wearing his colonial costume rather than a purple beret.

When the Kleins, the Simses, and Lydia began to make their excuses, leaving nearly full plates on the table, Charlotte poured fresh coffee into Ian's cup. "Please sit down and calm yourself. No one here is accusing you."

The other guests paused in their exodus, likely waiting to see how Ian would respond.

"Perhaps no one is verbalizing condemnation," Ian blurted. "But their faces and avoidance speak far more than mere words could ever say—"

"As a courtesy to your kind hostess, maybe you could cease and desist," Lydia said, her quiet voice slicing through his rhetoric.

Ian's eyes widened, as if that had never occurred to him. He paused. "I bow to her humanity and sense of justice." He sat and drank his coffee without further comment.

Charlotte, stifling a sigh of relief at Ian's silence, circulated among the guests, offering seconds and bits of conversation. Perhaps this breakfast might end on a positive note after all.

She was glad to see that Lydia, contrary to her usual custom, lingered with a second cup of Earl Grey. Although Charlotte was concerned that she ate only a few bites.

Charlotte was dismayed to notice that Daniel didn't attack his breakfast like he normally did and Maggie seemed quieter than usual. She wondered what was upsetting the couple.

After pushing aside their plates, Tom and Bonnie pulled needles and yarn from their totes and began knitting matching red-and-blue winter hats, a cozy activity that seemed to both soothe and cheer the group.

Although the remainder of breakfast was uneventful, Charlotte didn't mind the serenity that settled into the room when the guests finally dispersed. After cleaning up and washing the dishes, Charlotte contemplated sitting on the veranda. Maybe the lake breezes had counteracted the August sun's heat, keeping the temperature bearable.

Charlotte had just entered the foyer when the bell chimed and the front door opened.

A fiftyish man wearing a cream-colored linen suit strode toward her, a frown stamped on his dark, handsome face. "Are Magdalena and Daniel Sims staying at this inn?"

And hello to you too. Charlotte forced a welcoming smile. "Good morning, Mr.—"

"I am John Paul Gutiérrez, Magdalena's father, and I demand to know whether she is here."

Demand? Instead of folding her arms and glaring as she wanted to, Charlotte gripped the edge of the front desk. "I'm sorry, but I can't tell you if your daughter is here or not. We respect our guests' privacy."

"That is absurd." His face reddened. "I must speak with the owner."

Charlotte curled her lips in what she hoped was a maddening smile. "I am the owner."

"Impossible," he said. "You are too young."

"Thank you for the compliment." Charlotte widened her grin. "I wish I could help, but I'm afraid I cannot accommodate you."

"How dare you refuse a father's wishes!" John Paul roared. "I am only concerned for my daughter's safety." His face turned a dusky purple. "I have heard that thieves run wild in this town and your inn is unsafe."

"Sir, we have suffered the loss of one embroidered sampler." Charlotte wasn't about to mention Dean's clock. "That hardly makes the inn unsafe." Now she crossed her arms. "Can I help you with anything else?"

"You will regret your lack of cooperation," he threatened. "I shall call my lawyers. I shall—"

"Papa?" Maggie's childlike voice sounded even more so in the wake of her father's rage.

Charlotte turned to see Daniel and Maggie standing stock-still at the top of the stairs.

"Papa!" Maggie's face darkened to a similar purple as she stormed downstairs to glare into his face. "What are you doing here?"

"You thought I would not find you, but I have my ways," John Paul said. He had lowered his voice, but his tone fed the flames in his daughter's eyes. "I spent a fortune so you could have your dream wedding and your special honeymoon. A good daughter would have been grateful. Instead, you ran away. You did not tell me where you were going."

"This is exactly why we didn't," Daniel said, his boyish face hardening to stone.

John Paul scowled at him. "I have talked with the townspeople. How can you place my only daughter in danger like this?"

Daniel descended the stairs and put an arm around his wife. He towered over his father-in-law. "Maggie is not in danger. She's safe with me."

Charlotte gulped. The easygoing young man had disappeared, and in his place, a man with a dangerous gleam in his eye glowered.

"You?" John Paul scoffed. "She's not safe with you."

"I will take care of Maggie," Daniel said through gritted teeth. "She's my wife."

It only escalated from there. Maggie shouted defiance, her father shouted back, and Daniel looked scarier by the minute.

Charlotte was on the verge of calling the police when John Paul delivered what sounded like his final threats.

"I'll cut you out of the will," he said. "You know I have many friends in high places, and I will not hesitate to call them."

"You're not in Texas," Daniel reminded him, his blue eyes blazing. "Call all the friends you want."

John Paul stared through him. "You both should be glad I have such friends."

Maggie blanched.

"Go ahead and write us out of your will," Daniel said. "Maggie and I are staying here, as we planned. If you don't go home right now, we might never return to Texas."

"Here?" John Paul spat. "You would stay *here*?"

Charlotte bristled. How dare he put down their inn?

"How will you make a new life? You have no money," John Paul said, then blustered out more intimidation. Finally, he turned on his heel and stormed away, slamming the front door.

Maggie closed her eyes and muttered something Charlotte couldn't quite pick up.

Daniel glared after his father-in-law, muscles twitching in his still-set jaw.

Charlotte didn't know what to say. There were no helpful hints in the innkeeper's handbook to deal with something like this.

"I'm sorry Papa was rude to you and caused such a scene," a subdued Maggie said to Charlotte. Then she exchanged a glance with Daniel that Charlotte couldn't interpret. "He'll go home, and Mama will make it all better."

Charlotte was still speechless.

Maggie tugged on her husband's arm. "Come on. Let's go kayaking before it gets too hot."

Daniel wore a stony expression. "Sure. But if your dad paddles after us—"

"I'll let you dump him into the lake." Maggie gave him a ghost of her usual smile. "As long as you don't drown him."

"Don't tempt me," Daniel said.

Maggie took his hand and led him toward the back veranda.

Charlotte sighed. She needed some quiet time and a gallon of iced tea. She went to the kitchen and poured herself a tall glass. Then she retreated to the veranda and sat down.

Soon Winston appeared and jumped onto her lap.

Charlotte smiled as she hugged the sweet little dog. He seemed to know that she needed comfort.

Charlotte was still sitting on the veranda, gazing at the lake with Winston, when she heard footsteps.

Grace poked her head out the door. "I'm home. Did you have a nice, peaceful morning?"

Charlotte stretched in her comfy living room chair, contemplating her carefully manicured toes resting on an equally comfy ottoman.

After hearing about Charlotte's stressful morning, Grace had shooed her home for the afternoon. Despite writing deadlines, Charlotte decided that with the commotion of the festival, a major party, and two thefts, she should give herself time off as well. Already, the serene decor of her cottage was soothing her into drowsiness . . .

Charlotte thought she'd dreamed the timid knock. But when it came again a little louder, she got up and trudged over to the front door. Grace had willingly shouldered inn duty this afternoon. Why couldn't whoever this was approach her instead of interrupting Charlotte's nap?

When she checked the peephole, the sight of a sad-eyed Maggie banished her sleepiness. Charlotte opened the door. "Are you all right? Can I help you with something?"

The young woman twisted a dark curl. "I feel terrible about this morning. I wanted to apologize again for Papa's rudeness."

"Sometimes dads get a little overprotective." That was the understatement of the year, but seeing Maggie's eyes well with tears, Charlotte brushed off the man's outrageous behavior.

"It was the first time I didn't have Mama around to calm him down." A tear trickled down Maggie's smooth, caramel-colored cheek. "I didn't help things by yelling at him."

Charlotte couldn't believe that Maggie was blaming herself. A spurt of outrage heated her sympathy, but she kept it out of her voice. "Would you like to come in and have a glass of tea?"

Maggie hesitated. "I don't want to bother you."

"It's no bother at all," Charlotte assured her. She felt terrible for Maggie and wanted to help if she could. Married less than two weeks, this young newlywed was already tangling with tough problems—without her mama.

Upon entering the cottage, Maggie's face brightened. "The inn's beautiful, but I love your house. It's so warm and friendly."

They talked about interior decorating as Charlotte poured the tea. Maggie said that she and Daniel had attempted to furnish their first apartment on a shoestring budget. "I didn't want to ask Papa for money, but he bought us a bunch of living room furniture anyway. It's all too big and fancy. Daniel hates it." Her voice broke.

"I'm sorry," Charlotte said.

Maggie bit her lip. "This morning, I was so afraid Daniel and Papa were going to get into a fight."

Charlotte had thought they would too, but she said, "Both of them love you."

The bride's eyes shone through her tears, and she smiled. "Daniel does, or he wouldn't have put up with Papa all this time." Her smile faded. "I think Papa loves controlling people more than anything."

From what Charlotte had seen and heard, it was probably true, but she said, "Some men have trouble expressing themselves. Your father may think pouring money out on you shows that he loves you."

"Maybe." Maggie stared into her glass. "I guess a little love might hide somewhere under all that 'family pride,' as he calls it." Her voice sank to a whisper. "Especially since I haven't done much to make him proud."

Charlotte didn't know how to respond so she remained silent.

Maggie thumped her drink on the end table and leaped to her feet. "Thanks for the tea. I'm sorry, but I really have to go." She slipped outside.

Charlotte hurried to the front door. Should she call after Maggie? Try to follow her?

She took too long to decide. Maggie sprinted away, her shoulders heaving as she ran.

Grace

If Grace stayed underwater, maybe Ian wouldn't find her.

That was probably not a good idea. Bubbles fizzed around Grace as she broke the lake's surface and stroked through the clear, slightly tepid water. At least if she remained a fair distance from shore, he'd have to swim or kayak to reach her.

Ian had knocked on her door about some imaginary malfunction of the air-conditioning in his suite. The so-called emergency had dissolved any chance of her going to the festival. By hospitality hour, she was feeling a bit inhospitable.

Maggie had complicated Charlotte's Sunday afternoon too. Despite that, her sister had recruited friendly Mimi, whom they'd invited to hospitality hour with her husband, Doug, to help distract Ian. Afterward, Grace had slipped into her private quarters to change into her swimsuit, then escaped out the door and made her way to the lake.

Now, floating under the sunset's spectacular sky, Grace gave thanks for each peaceful breath. The guests this time around seemed to need far more than they could provide. She had no idea how God handled all His children's quirks and failings.

Amid prayers for strength and patience, she spotted the silhouette of a tall man on the inn's pier.

Before she could dive underwater again, the figure whistled, and a large dog loped to his side for a thorough petting.

Spencer and his chocolate Labrador retriever, Bailey.

"Hey!" Spencer called to Grace. "Want a frozen lemonade? Or are you too cold for one?"

"No, this water's as warm as a bathtub." Grace swam to the pier. As she climbed the ladder, she teased Bailey. "Watch out. I'm going to shake on you."

Spencer laughed. "We won't mind cooling off, will we, Bailey?"

The dog barked as if in response.

Grace splatted water from her bathing suit onto both of them, then donned a terry cloth robe that would have proved too warm but for the chilly treat Spencer offered. She held it against her cheek. "This is perfect. Thank you."

He smiled. "Always tastes better when I share one with a friend."

They walked along the shoreline with Bailey trotting ahead of them. Grace and Spencer occasionally remarked on the beautiful evening, the week's weather report, and the palatial homes that fronted one part of the lake. Half the time, they strolled without saying anything.

Only when the darkening sky lit up with gold, blue, and red fireworks did they acknowledge the Candlelight Journey Festival—and its end.

"Though it's not over for you, is it?" A fresh burst of fiery blossoms lit the concern on Spencer's face. "You still have to deal with the theft of your sampler."

"You're right about that." Grace sighed. "Were you there when Dean realized his clock had been stolen?"

"No, but I heard about it. I also heard the police are leaning pretty hard on Ian."

Don't let Ian lean on you. Spencer didn't say that, but the tightening of his voice held a note of warning.

"When you work with people, there are always challenges," Grace said lightly. "Charlotte and I will get through it like we always do."

"You will," he said. "But don't hesitate to ask me for help."

"You've already helped so much." *Even if you didn't come to our party.* She dabbed a spoonful of lemonade on her tongue, savoring its tart sweetness.

Spencer shrugged off the compliment. "Just wanted you to know you can always give me a call."

His smile hinted that if she called, he might come running. That made a tough end to the festival and Sunday a whole lot better.

Monday morning, Grace hurried to the foyer when she heard the bell above the front door jingle.

Winston raced past her and bounded over to Captain Daley.

The captain leaned down to pet Winston, then greeted Grace. "I'd like to have another word with Dr. Southby. Is he here?"

Did the purposeful expression on Daley's face bode well or ill? Grace couldn't tell. "Yes, he's in here." She ushered him to the music room.

"Dr. Southby, you didn't mention you were once arrested for stealing several copies of first editions from a museum," the captain said without preamble.

Grace smothered a gasp.

Ian's face whitened, but he recovered quickly. "The books were not first editions. The museum's copy of Charles Dickens's *Great Expectations* was published in 1864, the original book in 1861. The copy of *A Boy's Will* by Robert Frost was published in 1917, the original in 1913. His book, *North of Boston,* was published in—"

"You stole several valuable books from the Apperson Museum in Illinois, didn't you?" Daley interrupted.

Ian raised his chin. "Yes, but I had excellent reasons for doing so."

The captain paused as if to gain control, then said, "Apparently, you served no jail time in Illinois. But here, we view theft as a serious offense."

"I do not doubt that, but you are wasting your time," Ian retorted. "Have you found evidence to incriminate me?"

"No," Daley admitted. "But we do ask that you remain in the area, pending further investigation."

"I had already determined that in the face of unjust suspicion, I shall not run away. I shall stay until vindicated."

Grace tried not to wince at his promise to stay indefinitely.

"Just keep it on the straight and narrow," the captain said, then turned to Grace. "May I speak with you privately for a moment?"

"Of course." She led him to the living room.

"How much do you know about Lydia Walkerton?" Daley asked.

Grace couldn't hide her surprise. Why was the captain asking about Lydia? It didn't seem possible that the woman could be a suspect in the thefts, not when she hardly left her room. "She keeps to herself most of the time. I only know what she's told us, which isn't much."

"What has she told you?"

"She's a fashion designer from New York." She hesitated, then volunteered, "She appeared quite troubled from the moment she arrived."

"Her background has checked out," the captain said, "but we found that she was also arrested at one time."

Grace's mouth went dry. "Why?"

"It happened a long time ago when she was a teen," Daley said. "She went joyriding with friends in a relative's car without permission. Her wealthy family managed to get her probation, and she hasn't had so much as a parking ticket since. Still, I thought you should know."

"Anything else?" Grace asked, bracing herself for more disheartening news.

"Daniel and Maggie Sims were both arrested once for underage drinking," he answered.

Grace remembered what Charlotte had told her about Maggie's visit to the cottage. Was that why the young woman seemed to think she deserved her father's harsh treatment?

"Tom and Bonnie Klein didn't show up in any of our databases," the captain continued. "For now, I'm not planning to focus on the other guests. But if you notice anything unusual, no matter how small, please report it to me."

Grace nodded and walked him to the door.

The captain had just left when Grace's phone rang.

It was Patty Duncan. "I need a favor in the worst way."

"How can I help you?" Grace asked.

"All festival long, I've been thinking about how to fix things between Winnie and me. I've missed her so much," Patty said. She sounded tearful. "Will you help me? Just do this one little thing for The Busy Bees meeting tomorrow night."

Grace had forgotten about the meeting. Given the bizarre weekend, she'd almost forgotten about the quarrel between Winnie and Patty. "What can I do for you?"

"Bring the gowns you and Charlotte wore to your party," Patty replied.

Exactly what will that accomplish? Even though Grace had doubts about the plan, she agreed to bring the gowns.

"Oh, thank you!" Patty exclaimed.

By the time she hung up, Grace had given up figuring out Patty's logic. She rejected all thoughts of Lydia's arrest history, Maggie's family problems, or any other troubles. Her mind refused to wrap itself around Ian's vow that he wouldn't leave until proven innocent.

She'd hoped the week would improve, but it seemed to be

getting worse instead. A Monday morning like this called for extreme cleaning therapy.

After she finished scrubbing all the bathrooms, Grace decided to take a walk with Winston by the lake. She'd leave her phone at home and speak to no one.

Usually she enjoyed running into friends. The more talkative, the better.

But this morning, she hoped nobody stopped her. If they did, Grace feared the words that might escape her mouth.

Fluffy clouds floating through blue heavens peeked at Grace and Winston through mossy canopies of green leaves. Sunbeams waltzed with the lake's gentle waves.

The primeval rhythms of this path had soothed Grace before, but half an hour passed before her steps slowed to match the music of the forest. Winston matched her pace.

As they walked, she heard two sets of footsteps approaching. Instinctively, she ducked behind a clump of bushes and held the little dog close. She was glad Winston remained quiet.

One voice belonged to a man she didn't recognize.

The other voice belonged to a woman she did. It was Lydia. However, her guest's clipped tone had risen to a volume Grace had never heard from the usually reticent designer.

"What are you doing here?" Lydia asked.

"You already know the answer to that question," the man said.

"Of course I do," Lydia sneered. "You want money."

Peering between branches, Grace saw that her ladylike guest who, though much smaller than the burly young man, looked like she would happily dig her manicured nails into his bearded face.

The two walked out of earshot, still arguing.

Shaken, Grace considered running home and calling the police. But what would she say? Her guest and the unknown man were quarreling about money? That wasn't a crime. His Eastern accent sounded like Lydia's, rather than local. Why had he followed her all the way to South Carolina?

Instead of informing the police, Grace picked up Winston and trailed the combatants, hoping to learn more. But they'd lowered the volume on their unpleasant exchange, making it harder for Grace to follow.

When their voices faded to nothing, Grace skirted the area. She searched farther along the path, hoping to chance upon the man who had made Lydia so angry. He'd been dressed casually in jeans, a T-shirt, and heavy work shoes.

The last kind of person she'd expect Lydia to know.

Despite his size, he seemed to have vanished. Grace considered asking at a business or two in town, but she'd have to explain her interest. With the festival's end and little to talk about, the Magnolia Harbor grapevine would certainly pounce on that juicy tidbit.

She did spot Lydia, standing on the path alone, as immobile as a statue. When she remained staring at the lake, Grace set Winston down and deliberately rustled a few branches along the path.

Lydia started, then chilled her with an arctic gaze.

Grace forced a smile. "Lovely day for a walk along the lake, isn't it?"

Winston wagged his tail as if in agreement.

Lydia gave a barely perceptible nod. Blue flames glimmered in her eyes as if encased in ice.

"Sometimes being out in nature helps me think things through," Grace said, trying again. "Gain a new perspective."

Lydia curled her lip, but a mangled sob escaped from her throat that seemed to startle her as much as it did Grace. "Why?" she asked, then fled in the opposite direction.

Running after her probably wouldn't solve anything.

The serene lapping of the lake's gentle waves seemed to mock Grace as she tried to decipher what had just happened.

Grace attempted to push away the encounter, but her serene walk was spoiled. With Winston trotting beside her, she reentered the woods and turned back toward the inn.

But she couldn't ignore the possibilities that poked at her tired brain. Did the stranger have anything to do with the thefts of the sampler and the clock? But the enormous young man would have stood out at both the Magnolia Harbor Inn and The Tidewater. Grace would have remembered him. Surely someone else would have noticed his presence. Maybe he'd driven a getaway car?

How did Lydia fit into his scheme?

Or, given Lydia's odd dominance, how had he fit into hers?

Winnie

"Mom, you can't let this costume thing keep you caged up like this," Paisley insisted.

"Nobody's put me in a cage," Winnie said, setting a plate of huckleberry cobbler on the table in front of her youngest daughter. "I decided not to go to the festival. My decision. No one else's."

It definitely wasn't the town council's decision. And no matter what the mayor's niece thought, she didn't rule the roost.

Paisley peered over her coffee mug. "So you put yourself in a cage?"

"Watch your tongue," Winnie said as she sat down at the table with her own plate. She'd taken a tiny piece of cobbler for herself. "I didn't raise you to sass your elders."

"I don't mean any disrespect." Paisley put her mug down. "I just hate to see you so unhappy. You haven't gone anywhere lately."

"I helped Grace and Charlotte at their party," Winnie reminded her. "And I went to Dean's bash. How can you say I haven't gone anywhere?"

"But you didn't go on the Candlelight Journey with Grace or Charlotte—or us," Paisley said. "Everybody wanted to know if you were sick. You missed church on Sunday, and Sam and Monica asked where you were."

Winnie cringed. She hated disappointing her grandchildren. "I wasn't feeling up to it," she muttered. It was the truth. Wasn't it?

"Dad said you didn't leave the house yesterday or today." Paisley still hadn't touched her cobbler. "When are you going to stop hiding out at home?"

Winnie stuffed a huge bite of cobbler into her mouth. Maybe while she chewed, she'd think of an answer. Instead, she choked.

Paisley pounded her on the back. "Are you all right?"

Winnie waved away her daughter's concern. "You don't realize it, but I'm getting older. Sometimes I'm tired."

Paisley narrowed her eyes. "I never knew old age to drop in on a person overnight," she said gently.

"That's because you're young."

Paisley sighed. "I can see I'm not making any headway here. I might as well eat this cobbler before I have to pick up the kids at school."

"Good. Don't waste your breath. Or my huckleberry cobbler."

Winnie smoothed her hair, trying to ignore the butterflies in her stomach at the thought of facing Patty. But maybe she wouldn't show up tonight.

"Are you going to Busy Bees?" Gus asked, glancing at his watch.

"I know I'm running late." Winnie grabbed her purse and keys. She had offered to take Grace, Bonnie, and Lydia to the meeting. Now she wished she hadn't.

"Have a good time." Gus kissed her cheek before retreating to the safety of his recliner and the TV.

When Winnie arrived at the inn, the women were waiting. "Sorry I'm late."

"Don't worry about it." Grace gave her a hug, then picked up a large tote bag.

Bonnie and Lydia collected their things and followed Winnie and Grace to the car.

While Winnie drove them to Spool & Thread, she told a few amusing stories about her cat, Phoebe. She hoped to cheer up Lydia. As usual, Lydia was dressed to the nines, but all the makeup in the world couldn't disguise the dark circles under her eyes and her sunken cheeks.

Grace and Bonnie laughed, and a smile crossed Lydia's pale face.

By the time they arrived, Lydia had relaxed some, and so had Winnie.

But when they entered the shop, loud laughter struck Winnie's ears like a cracked bell.

They were all laughing—Judith, Helen, Angel, and Patty. And a young dark-haired woman Winnie had never seen before. She must be Jillian, the mayor's niece, who had fired Winnie over the phone.

Judith greeted them with a smile. "Good evening, ladies. Please introduce your guest."

Winnie cast a longing look at the sewing machines, then took a deep breath. "I'm so happy Lydia Walkerton from New York City came tonight. Lydia, this is Judith Mason, who owns the shop. And Helen Daley and Angel Diaz."

They welcomed Lydia.

"And this is Patty Duncan," Winnie said, then turned to Jillian. "But I don't believe I've met you."

"I'm Jillian Price," the young woman said. "We talked over the phone—"

"So pleased to meet you face-to-face," Winnie said, cutting her off.

"Refreshments first tonight," Judith said brightly. She plopped a three-layer cake covered with pecans on the table and passed out plates. "Help yourselves to coffee or tea."

Even though Winnie wanted to sample the rich cake, she refrained because of her earlier cobbler indulgence. Instead, she poured herself a cup of coffee. She noted with satisfaction that Lydia was nibbling her piece. Maybe the woman would get her appetite back after all.

"So, Jillian and Patty, tell us about your play this past weekend," Judith said.

Winnie put down her cup.

Jillian hesitated. "Our audience the first night was small, but the second was better."

"You were amazing," Angel told Patty.

"Patty was great, and so were the rest of the actors." Jillian paused. "But several costumes were the wrong size or didn't work with the characters."

Patty nodded. "We had trouble with the changes between scenes too."

Winnie froze.

"The truth is," Patty continued, "we could have used professional help with the costumes." She motioned to Grace.

Winnie's niece magically produced the party gowns Winnie had made from her tote bag.

"I had Grace bring the outfits Winnie sewed for her and her sister," Patty told Jillian. "What do you think?"

Amid oohs and aahs from all the others, the ice deep in Winnie's bones began to thaw.

"I think I made a big mistake," Jillian said simply. She walked across the room to Winnie. "My job was to make the Candlelight Journey Festival the very best. The play would have gone so much better if I had recognized your skills and experience."

Winnie remained silent.

"I don't know if I'll be back in Magnolia Harbor anytime soon," Jillian went on. "But if I manage any other festivals within a hundred miles, I'd like to call on you." She stared Winnie straight in the eye. "May I?"

Winnie couldn't get a word out of her clogged throat. Melted ice in her bones was threatening to wash out of her eyes. She didn't dare glance at Lydia, who must wonder what this was all about. Winnie nodded, then nodded again.

Jillian held out her hand, and Winnie grasped it.

Patty burst into tears and threw her arms around Winnie. "I can't believe I thought we could do the festival without you. Jillian didn't know. I should have told her. But I got carried away with trying new stuff. I'm sorry. I'm so sorry."

Now the melted ice gushed down Winnie's cheeks. Thankfully, Patty was crying so hard that no one would notice Winnie's tears.

"You stop that right now," Winnie commanded, "or you'll drown both of us."

That made Patty laugh and cry.

Everyone else laughed and cried too.

When things finally quieted, Winnie said, "I should have talked it out with you. I should have been a better friend. I'm sorry too."

Later, under the cover of the usual small talk, Winnie turned to Lydia. "I'm sorry you had to see all this." What must Lydia think of them?

"No problem." A wistful smile curved her lips. "You're all good friends, aren't you?"

"The best." Sudden gratitude overwhelmed Winnie. "We get mad sometimes, but we've stuck together for a long time."

Now that tensions had eased, talk flowed like a spring. More oohs and aahs ensued when the others persuaded Grace to model the blue dress.

"I'll bet Spencer Lewis loved the sight of you," Judith teased.

Grace said nothing, but her eyes didn't quite match her smile.

Come to think of it, Winnie hadn't seen Spencer at the inn's bash. Why not? She knew he'd been invited.

Her thoughts were interrupted when Judith hauled out the quilts and sewing supplies. Winnie had forgotten Lydia was a designer. Goodness gracious, the woman could sew. She whipped together curved pieces as if they were straight edges.

With Lydia's help, they might even finish the baby quilts tonight. But Lydia appeared to be upset again. Winnie reviewed their conversations. Had someone said something wrong to Lydia? Had she herself said something wrong?

As they added batting and backing to the little quilts, Winnie tried to bring back Lydia's smile by telling more kitty stories.

But her new friend stayed quiet as she worked.

Winnie's pastel quilt with teddy bears on it had turned out even better than she'd hoped.

The others had noticed, and compliments filled the room.

"I hope the new mama likes it," Winnie said. *But this quilt's not for the hospital*, her inner voice said. *It's for Lydia.*

It wasn't the first time Winnie had felt that urge. Prompted by it, she'd offered others gifts that ranged from a screwdriver to a Bible.

But this quilt wasn't hers to give, though she knew the other quilters would understand. They'd witnessed her gifts before, articles that turned out to be exactly what the recipients needed. Besides, Winnie could whip up a similar quilt on her own well before the deadline.

Still, what would Lydia think? She could sew a quilt like this in record time. Did she have grandchildren? Winnie realized the designer hadn't mentioned her family at all.

Despite her questions, Winnie pressed the quilt and brought it to Lydia. "This is for you."

The woman choked. Her face turned fiery, then purple.

"Lydia!" Winnie dropped the quilt and reached to help her. "Are you all right? Call 911!"

Judith snatched up her phone.

"Don't call anyone," Lydia said in a tight, hoarse voice. "I'm fine."

"You're not fine," Winnie retorted. "What can we do to help you?"

Lydia pulled away as if Winnie's touch would burn her. Without another word, she stepped around both Winnie and the quilt and fled from the room.

15

Grace

Grace rushed to finish her bank business in the historic brick building in downtown Magnolia Harbor. She slipped in and out before anyone could talk to her about the thefts. Ditto for the Dragonfly Coffee Shop when she'd stopped in for a mocha.

Walking along the cobblestone street, Grace spotted Sophie Mah, the owner of Miss Millie's dress shop, through her front window. She would have loved to chat with Sophie, but Grace didn't want to rehash all the details of the thefts.

Reverend Glen Abrams exited Fellowship Christian Church. When he spotted Grace, he smiled and waved. "Good morning."

Grace greeted him with a smile.

"Sorry to run, but I have a meeting at the chamber of commerce," the pastor said. "I'll see you soon."

"No need to apologize," Grace said, trying to hide her relief. Watching him walk toward the quaint restored train station, she gave thanks for the inner strength that radiated from him, as solid and reassuring as their picturesque clapboard church with its steeple that watched over downtown.

As she avoided townspeople, Grace found herself searching for an excuse to stay away from the inn.

She bit her lip. Had she ever felt that way before? The inn was her home, her haven. She did her best to make it a sanctuary for everyone who stepped through the door.

Now, though, she needed a place to breathe.

Her walk along the lake path yesterday hadn't proved very relaxing. On passing the police station, Grace wondered again if she should stop and mention Lydia's arguing with the strange man.

Amid the debate with herself, the Heritage Library beckoned to her with its tall arched windows and majestic entrance. It was the perfect place to forget everything.

Grace scrambled up the marble steps and through the door.

Phyllis Gendel nodded and smiled. The head librarian stood behind the circulation desk. She was busy checking out a stack of books for a mother with three preschoolers, so there was no chance for a conversation with her at the moment.

Grace waved as she climbed the curved, ornate staircase to the stately second floor.

She breathed a sigh of relief. There was no one in sight. Sniffing the beloved fragrance of old books and lemon oil, she wondered if her blood pressure had dropped ten points already.

Grace grabbed a magazine—mostly for show if someone walked in—and headed for her chosen refuge, a comfortable old armchair hidden by rows of bookshelves. Sinking into its creaky depths, she basked in sunbeams shining through a window. She savored the view of the waterfront and lake, then closed her eyes.

"Grace?"

She opened her eyes and found Ian standing before her, holding a package wrapped in brown paper.

"Forgive me for disturbing you," he said, looking like an apologetic little boy.

Grace liked to think of herself as a kind person and a good listener. But right now, she didn't have the patience. "Have you been following me?" she blurted out.

Ian appeared stricken. "No, of course not. I decided to come here because I love libraries. When I saw you walk in, I thought maybe we could have some privacy. I could explain about the books I took from that museum."

Was Ian casing the place for another heist? Grace closed her eyes again. If only she could make him disappear like a fairy-tale villain with a magical wave of her hand.

But was he a villain?

No matter how tightly she shut her eyes, Grace couldn't erase the picture of Ian's gaze, unblinking and open.

Had he given her that look when he tried to buy the sampler for $49,000 less than what he knew it was worth?

Still, justice demanded that she listen to Ian's version of the museum thefts. Grace opened her eyes and motioned to a nearby chair. "Please take a seat."

"Thank you." Ian flung off his cape and dropped into the chair, placing his package on the floor. He straightened, eyeing her once more. "I took the books because they were not receiving the proper care of historical treasures."

Grace almost smiled. Yes, Ian would consider that a rescue operation.

"When I do research, I treat materials with the utmost respect," he continued. "Those editions, if handled by the public at all, should have required gloves and careful supervision. Instead, they'd been tossed haphazardly on a table. I caught children actually scribbling on them."

"I assume you spoke with the curator," Grace said.

"Naturally." Ian's face darkened, and his coal-colored eyes smoldered. "A moron! An imbecile who should not have been allowed to cross the museum's threshold, let alone manage it!"

The apologetic little boy Ian had resembled a few moments ago had morphed into a big, irate man who filled their nook.

Grace gripped the arms of her chair, but she could not take her eyes off the man's drastic transformation. "You should keep your voice down."

Ian complied, but his angry tone hardly lessened in intensity. "When that idiot showed no concern whatsoever, I took the books with me. It wasn't difficult, as he'd disappeared into a back room. I could have taken every artifact in the place if I had wanted. And don't think I was not tempted. History should be respected."

"What happened then?" Grace asked.

Ian clenched his fists. "When the curator realized the books were missing, he called the police. They questioned me at my hotel, and upon my confession, I was arrested."

She didn't know what to say.

"After all, justice had to be served." His voice oozed sarcasm. "However, instead of calling a lawyer, I contacted Mr. Whitlow, the president of the museum's board of directors."

"What did he do?"

"Mr. Whitlow investigated for himself, then convinced the board to fire that poor excuse for a curator." Ian shook his head. "It turned out the man was a relative of a former board member and had no historical background whatsoever."

"So the police dropped the charges?" Grace asked.

"Yes." Ian slowly unclenched his fists.

"Did you tell Captain Daley what you've just told me?"

"Do you think it would have mattered?" Ian demanded.

Grace resisted the urge to draw back. "Is it fair to assume he wouldn't believe you?"

Ian paused. "I suppose not," he said quietly. "But I hope that you will consider what I've told you a confidence. I wish to make up my own mind in that regard."

"I understand." She did, though he'd just added one more weight on her shoulders.

During the next few moments of silence, she watched some of the fury drain from his face. She hoped he was considering talking to Captain Daley.

"I suppose I should have told him something else," he muttered.

Another red flag. Grace didn't want to know something else, but did she have a choice?

"That night at The Tidewater party, I noticed Tom Klein standing near the clock collection." Ian's fists curled again. "When he thought no one was looking, he pocketed something."

She felt as if the air were being squeezed from her lungs. Tom? Sweet, slightly bumbling Tom? He would never have stolen Dean's clock.

"He's always pulling out his pocket watch," Grace reasoned. "Or he could have been making sure he had his car keys or his billfold. He's a bit absentminded."

"I don't think so," Ian replied. "Earlier Tom had mentioned that he'd moved his watch to his left pocket so he could still check the time. In the instance I describe, he used his bandaged hand—which, by the way, moved very quickly and efficiently after such a recent burn."

Grace stared, her mouth as dry as a desert. "You think he pretended to have an accident? But Bonnie was with him when he spilled his coffee. She took him to the emergency room."

"Did she?" Ian asked, studying her. "It's possible, but we only have their word for it."

Grace had a disturbing thought. Stealing the clock with a bandaged hand wouldn't have left fingerprints. Bile rose in her throat. Had Bonnie mentioned exactly where they were eating when Tom burned his hand? Whether she'd taken Tom to Magnolia Harbor's Northshore Medical Center or somewhere else?

Grace's sensible side urged her to call Patty. She was a physical therapist at the hospital, so she could find out if Tom had been treated there. But that would have been asking her to breach patient confidentiality, and Grace couldn't put her friend in that position.

She tried to still her writhing stomach. Even if Tom hadn't been treated there, it certainly wouldn't prove his wrongdoing. But it would open up the possibility that Ian's absurd notion was right.

Grace shifted her weary gaze to the window. She didn't know how long she sat there, lost in a choking fog that devoured the sunshine.

The muffled crunch of paper interrupted her reverie, and she glanced up.

"So sorry. I didn't mean to startle you," Ian said. The little boy had returned. "But I brought you a gift. One I hope you won't refuse." He handed her the package.

She fought a sigh. Who else but Ian would choose this moment to bestow an unwanted present on her? Then panic flooded her veins as she considered the situation. How had he known he would see her downtown? Perhaps he had stalked her after all.

"I thought I made it clear I do not expect hostess gifts from my guests," Grace reminded him.

He stared down at his hands. "It is not a hostess gift. Not a romantic gift either—though I wish it could be."

There. He'd said it.

If only the old chair could send her as far away as childhood stories had taken her. Away from this perplexing man. Away from his gifts and bizarre ways and his pleading, riveting face.

Ian cleared his throat. "I know that for now at least it will not happen, so I searched for this as a gift between friends." His face colored a little. "I picked it up from a packaging store out by the interstate. Of course, I intended to wrap it properly and give it to you later. But now seems like the best time."

Too weary to protest, Grace exhaled. "All right."

At least the flat package probably didn't hold roses. It was too square for a book. Jewelry? Her limp hands could hardly undo the string and stiff paper. His strong ones helped open the box.

A sampler.

A small linen sampler with the alphabet, numbers, and the figure of a colonial girl, all stitched in faded reds and blues.

She opened her mouth, but nothing came out.

"I'm afraid it's not nearly as elaborate as the missing one," Ian said. "It was stitched by a younger girl. But Mary Ann Roberts learned her craft at the same school as Elizabeth Byrd, who sewed your sampler." He paused. "It wasn't nearly as expensive either. I could not replace the one you lost. But I hope this one will—temporarily, we hope—fill the empty space on your wall."

Grace gazed at the sampler and smiled. "Thank you."

He bolted her to the chair with one more penetrating look. "My pleasure." Then he was gone, his tall, caped figure striding out of sight.

Pausing outside the library, Grace knew she couldn't linger downtown any longer. Even without the robberies, she should be playing catch-up after the festival.

She took a deep, calming breath. The rest of the day couldn't possibly prove as disturbing as this morning.

Ian had said his piece. He wouldn't ambush her again today, would he?

But one glance at the sampler reminded her that no rational predictions applied to the historian's behavior.

Though it also recalled his sensitivity to her loss. Or was it one more effort to manipulate her feelings? To perpetuate the lie of his innocence?

Grace commanded herself to take deep breaths and think positively as she walked to her car and drove home.

When she arrived at the inn, it appeared that she had the place almost to herself. All the guests—except for Lydia—were gone, and when Grace stepped through the door, Charlotte headed to her cottage to work on her cookbook.

Winston greeted her, his tail wagging.

Grace smiled and scratched behind his ears. "Have you been a good boy? Would you like a treat?"

The dog yipped and danced around her feet.

Laughing, she headed to the kitchen. She was so thankful for Winston. He always made her feel better.

After giving him a dog biscuit, Grace decided to clean her apartment and launder sheets and towels. Maybe housework's everyday rhythms would help to ease her mind.

As soon as she entered her suite, she felt the tension start to melt away. Even when messy, her room's all-white decor refreshed her.

Grace carefully stowed Ian's gift on the shelf in her closet and shut the door, resisting the urge to lock it.

After she dusted and vacuumed, she went outside despite the heat. She picked a bouquet of zinnias to brighten her bedside and her outlook.

Calm again, Grace didn't realize how desperately she hoped to avoid the Kleins until Bonnie's perky voice surprised her in the laundry room. "Grace?"

She jumped and dropped the towel she'd been removing from the dryer.

"Goodness," Bonnie said. "I didn't mean to startle you."

It felt like when Ian had ambushed her at the library. "May I help you?" Grace asked weakly.

Bonnie clicked her tongue. "My dear, you look like you could use some help." She began folding towels at lightning speed.

"You don't have to do that," Grace protested.

Bonnie shook her head firmly. "Nonsense. I enjoy housekeeping. Besides, Tom's taking a nap before we go shopping, so I have some free time."

As Bonnie chatted away, Grace found herself relaxing. She relaxed even more when Bonnie, upon learning she'd skipped lunch, insisted on fixing her a delicious turkey club sandwich. Normally Grace wouldn't have dreamed of allowing a guest to do such a thing, but she was emotionally exhausted and Bonnie's voice had taken on that no-nonsense tone only a mother could master.

While she ate, Grace's mind replayed a background video of Ian that morning. With each repeat, his caped appearance seemed more ridiculous, his claims about Tom even more so. How could the Kleins, some of the most pleasant guests she and Charlotte had ever hosted, steal from them? And from Dean?

Her doubts grew when Bonnie confided how thankful she was that Tom's accident with the hot coffee hadn't aggravated his blood pressure too much.

"I'm sure it's partly due to his feeling at home here," Bonnie said. "We're having such a wonderful, relaxing time." Despite her positive words, small worry wrinkles gathered on her forehead.

"Is something wrong?" Grace prompted.

Bonnie hesitated. "I've been debating whether to mention this or not. I definitely don't want to say anything to the police about it. At least not yet. I don't want to point a finger at an innocent man."

Grace set down her iced tea. "Please tell me what's troubling you."

She bit her lip. "When we were at Dean's party, Tom and I noticed Ian hovering around the collections, especially that clock grouping. Then, when I came out of the restroom, I saw him slip something under his cape. He always wears a cape, you know."

Grace's mental video of the historian froze. Yes, she knew.

Bonnie hurried on. "Maybe he's just one of those people who pilfer food at exclusive gatherings. Some do, even if they're well off."

"Yes, we've encountered one or two." She and Charlotte had once hosted an eccentric millionaire who not only had swiped hors d'oeuvres during hospitality hour but filched towels, boxes of tissues, and toilet paper.

"I certainly hope so," Bonnie said fervently. "Ian is a really nice man, and he's so intelligent and interesting."

Grace nodded, her mind whirling. Her appetite gone, she put the rest of her sandwich in the fridge.

Bonnie helped Grace straighten the living room. After ordering Grace not to skip any more meals, Bonnie went to awaken Tom from his nap so they could go shopping.

Dazed, Grace returned to her apartment. Before she could return her keys to their hook, Ian's gift drew her to the closet.

Taking it down from the shelf, she scrutinized its simple yet skilled needlework. Did he expect her to hang it on the wall today?

But how could she when Bonnie's revelation played and replayed at the same time as Ian's? The loops of both videos intertwined, tangling as Grace tried to make sense of what she'd heard.

She stowed the sampler back in the closet.

Today was out of the question.

Maybe she'd never hang it.

Charlotte

Charlotte stared at her laptop and sighed. She couldn't stop thinking about the thefts, and it was wrecking her train of thought.

She needed a break from working on her cookbook, and Grace could probably use her help.

Charlotte locked her cottage's front door when she left. Until the police arrested the thief—she glared at Ian's third-story windows—she would continue to be extra cautious.

When Charlotte entered the inn, Winston raced over and gave her a big doggy smile.

She couldn't help but smile in return. "Hey, boy, where's Grace?"

As if in answer, Winston trotted up the stairs.

Charlotte followed the dog to the second floor, where she found Grace dragging out the vacuum again. Charlotte knew better than to say the carpet looked fine to her because Grace seemed stressed.

Instead, Charlotte gestured toward the stairs. "I'm dying for a glass of tea. Come on. I'll pour you one too."

"I already took a break with Bonnie," Grace said as she yanked hoses and attachments off the vacuum.

Charlotte frowned. Why was Grace upset? Bonnie brightened everyone's day. "There's no law against spending quality time with your little sister. Especially if she'll vacuum for you."

That offer did the trick. Grace dropped the vacuum and said, "Let's go."

The sisters headed downstairs to the kitchen with Winston on their heels.

Charlotte retrieved a pitcher of tea from the fridge and poured two glasses. "So what's going on?"

Grace plopped down onto one of the stools. "It's been quite a day."

"What happened?" Charlotte set the glasses on the island and pulled up a stool.

Grace sipped her tea as she related Ian's appearance at the library and the story of his prior arrest. "Then he accused Tom of stealing Dean's clock."

"Tom?" Charlotte repeated, stunned. She was even more stunned by the way Grace seemed to take Ian's absurd claim seriously. Had the man cast some spell over her sister, vaporizing her brain?

When Grace told her Bonnie's account, it made perfect sense. Trying to be diplomatic, Charlotte said as much.

"If Ian did steal our sampler, why would he steal again?" Grace reasoned. "That would make him look even more guilty."

"It's not like the guy follows any sense of logic," Charlotte countered. "Maybe he's a kleptomaniac."

"It's possible."

Charlotte didn't miss the spot of color that bloomed on her sister's cheeks. "Why are you defending him? Did he give you roses again?"

She meant it as sarcasm, but when she looked into Grace's eyes, Charlotte knew. Roses or not, the historian had wormed his way into her sister's heart. "What did Ian do that makes you believe him? Did he give you something else?"

Grace slowly nodded. "Come and see." She led the way to her private quarters, then retrieved a box from the closet shelf and opened it. A sampler.

Charlotte caught her breath.

"He told me it's not nearly as valuable as the stolen sampler," Grace said.

Charlotte frowned, but she was glad that at least he hadn't tried to pull a con again.

"Still," Grace insisted, "he took the time to find one that was stitched by a girl who learned the craft at the same school as the girl who sewed ours."

"Ian may be strange, but he's also clever," Charlotte said. "He knew exactly what would get you on his side."

"Maybe." Grace returned the sampler to the closet. "Maybe not."

"You've got to be kidding. Do you really believe him?"

"I don't know what to believe."

"Don't you think someone objective ought to check out Ian's story before you accept it?" Charlotte asked.

Grace's mouth tightened. "He doesn't think the police will listen to him."

Charlotte resisted the urge to roll her eyes. Obviously, Grace had caved to Ian and decided not to inform Captain Daley.

Maybe Charlotte should tell the captain herself. But whether Ian's story turned out to be true or false, would Grace forgive her for betraying her trust? For sticking her nose into their guest's personal business?

As she mulled over the situation, an idea occurred to her. It wasn't a great idea, but it was better than letting Grace continue to believe Ian.

Charlotte measured her words carefully. "I'll bet Spencer could find out—off the record, of course—whether Ian's telling the truth about the museum heist."

A flicker of light in Grace's eyes quickly froze. "I don't think he'd be interested."

"I know he doesn't care for Ian," Charlotte remarked. Anyone with eyes could see that Spencer considered the historian competition for

Grace. "But he's your good friend. He knows all this is hard on you. And regardless if Ian's guilty or innocent, Spencer's a lawman at heart. He'll find out the truth."

Grace's set jaw told Charlotte she was getting nowhere.

"Look, this needs to be resolved," she persisted. "You can't take it anymore. If you won't call Spencer, then I will."

Grace's eyes hardened. "No."

Charlotte ignored her and yanked her phone from her pocket.

"Maybe you're right," Grace said and dropped her head.

Charlotte knew her sister feared losing Spencer's friendship. And Ian's. But they had to uncover the truth.

Grace pulled out her own phone and hit speed dial.

She brightened momentarily at hearing Spencer's voice, but soon her face clouded as she explained her reason for calling.

From her side of the conversation, Charlotte could tell Spencer had agreed to research Ian's story. She gave Grace a thumbs-up.

After Grace disconnected, she bit her lip. "He sounded so official. Like a detective interviewing a really dumb witness."

"No one thinks you're dumb." Charlotte hugged her. "Has it occurred to you that maybe Spencer wanted to help you all along? That maybe he was just waiting for you to ask?"

"Well, he has offered a couple of times." Grace relaxed a little. "So I guess I wasn't too out of line. Still, I doubt he's crazy about helping prove Ian's innocence."

Innocence? Charlotte didn't see that as a problem. Spencer would soon find evidence the man had lied, and Grace never could tolerate a liar.

For now, Charlotte gave her sister another hug, thankful she'd talked her into taking a positive step forward.

Grace turned toward the kitchen. "Do I hear someone at the back door?"

The knocking sounded more like an assault.

"Who on earth?" Grace hurried to the door and opened it.

Charlotte rushed after her and saw Dean standing there. His fiery face matched his dark-red tie. Even during a particularly chaotic weekend dinner rush at Le Crabe Fou, Charlotte had never seen him like this, with sweat dripping down his face, his normally perfect hair tousled, and his eyes blazing.

Grace summoned her usual smile. "Well, hello. Can we help you with something?"

He glared at them as if they'd conspired against him. "You certainly can. You can kick that thief out of your inn and help me run him out of town."

"Who are you referring to?" Grace asked.

"I'm talking about Ian," Dean snapped. "The con man who stole your sampler and my clock. Who else?"

Grace's smile disappeared. "We are not going to kick Ian or any other guest out of our inn. At least not until absolute proof has been found of his wrongdoing."

Charlotte would have been happy to comply, but she didn't care for Dean's demands. He hadn't blown up like this, even when he discovered the missing clock. Why was he so upset now? Who did he think he was, barging into their inn and talking to them like this? "We're very sorry your clock was stolen, but—"

"If you hadn't let him remain here, no place within a hundred miles would tolerate him," Dean interrupted. "Bottom line, you two are responsible for his presence in Magnolia Harbor—and at my inn this afternoon."

Grace stared at him. "What are you talking about?"

"He showed up in his ridiculous outfit while I was out on the water," Dean snapped. "He was annoying my guests, asking them questions about the theft—as if they aren't antsy enough. But that's not all. I caught him checking out my clock collection again."

Amid her own incredulity, Charlotte couldn't help but glance at Grace. *See?*

"You know we have no control over what our guests do when they're away from our inn," Grace said stiffly.

"Obviously." Dean glowered. "If he shows up at The Tidewater again, I'll call the police." He turned on his heel and marched out the door.

A moment later, they watched his silver car peel out of the driveway with a roar.

"Perhaps Dean should remember the police asked Ian to remain in the area," Grace said.

Charlotte agreed with Dean's assessment of the historian. Like The Tidewater owner, she feared Ian's thievery would hurt their business. But Dean's irrational accusations today puzzled her.

She and Dean had clashed often, but he tended to be sneaky, not belligerent. Storming and yelling wasn't like Dean at all.

Grace echoed her thoughts. "I don't understand him."

"I don't either." Charlotte shrugged. "I'm sick of this whole mess. I'm going to vacuum. Then I'm going to the Dragonfly for some heavy-duty caffeine. With double whipped cream."

"I feel like beating the daylights out of some rugs," Grace admitted. "And any pillow that gets in my way."

"Sounds like a plan." Charlotte slipped an arm around Grace's shoulders. "Let's forget about all this for today, okay? Maybe things will make sense tomorrow."

"I doubt it," Grace scoffed. But a little smile lit her face as they declared an unofficial truce.

"You came at the perfect time," Angel told Charlotte as she swiped the Dragonfly Coffee Shop's counter with a cloth. "It's the quietest afternoon we've had since before the festival."

Only a few strangers sipped drinks, all hypnotized by tablets or phones.

"I can handle quiet," Charlotte said as she breathed in the aroma of coffee. "And I'll take your largest vanilla latte. Double whipped cream, please."

"You got it." Angel expertly concocted the drink and brought it to Charlotte's table.

"Can you sit with me for a few minutes?" Charlotte asked.

"I always have time for a break with a favorite customer, especially when she looks upset." Angel grinned as she slid into the opposite chair. "How are things back at the inn?"

Charlotte grimaced. "At the moment, I'd rather forget the inn."

"Then you probably need to talk about it." Angel pantomimed zipping her lip. "As of now, this conversation never officially happened."

"That works," Charlotte said with a smile. Between sips of invigorating coffee, she told her friend about Ian's attempt to incriminate Tom.

Angel raised her eyebrows. "Tom? Tom Klein? I can't believe that for a minute. Why, he and Bonnie are the sweetest couple you'd ever meet. They come in here all the time." She paused and stared down at the table. "But . . ."

"But what?" Charlotte asked, leaning forward.

"Well, this morning, they got so mad at each other that I thought I'd have to blow a whistle to separate them. Especially Bonnie." Angel shook her head. "She was downright scary."

Charlotte sat back. Was she really talking about Bonnie? The woman was kind, and her eyes never lacked a twinkle. Maybe all the tensions at the inn were catching. "I've never seen the Kleins argue."

She grinned. "Mostly because Tom does whatever Bonnie says."

"Yeah, he does." Angel chuckled too. "But this morning, he wouldn't back down. I couldn't hear what they were fighting about, but he finally got up from the table and left her alone."

"Tom walked out?" Charlotte asked. She tried to picture the scene, but she couldn't.

Angel nodded. "He headed for the men's room and stayed in there for a long time. Bonnie waited, and after a while, she asked one of the male customers to check on him."

"What happened then?"

"Tom came out, still mad, but by that time, Bonnie had morphed back into a sweet old lady." Angel laughed. "Soon she was leading him around again."

Charlotte laughed too, but Tom and Bonnie's uncharacteristic quarrel reminded her of how she and Grace had clashed about Ian. And how, in the middle of their battle, Dean had blown them both away with his odd outburst. She told Angel about the conflicts.

"I hope it's not something in the drinking water," Angel remarked. "Even your honeymooners got bent out of shape yesterday."

"Daniel and Maggie?" Charlotte asked. She couldn't hide her surprise. They'd been inseparable ever since they arrived.

"Yes. I saw them walking down Main Street, and they were definitely not holding hands."

They were probably still upset about her father's interference. Charlotte tried to lighten up. "Maybe it's the full moon. I hope I don't find Lydia Walkerton howling with coyotes tonight."

Angel chuckled, then grew serious as she asked, "You and Grace are all right, aren't you?"

"Of course we are. We're sisters." *We have to be all right.* Charlotte stirred her latte a little too vigorously.

"Good. And I don't know what's bothering Dean, but I'm sure he won't stay mad very long."

"I don't care if he does." Charlotte took a sip of coffee, ignoring the skeptical look Angel gave her.

At hospitality hour, when Charlotte served Tom and Bonnie lemon-dill shrimp and roasted asparagus, they seemed as amiable as ever. In fact, Bonnie clung to Tom's uninjured arm even more than usual.

Apparently, the elderly lovebirds had patched things up. The young honeymooners didn't show, so Charlotte had no idea how they were doing.

As Charlotte headed to the kitchen to replenish the platters, she wondered if Dean had calmed down, then told herself it was none of her concern. After today's blowup, she wouldn't miss him if he decided to give her and Grace the silent treatment. After all, he'd caused plenty of trouble in their relationship.

But she had to admit that he had his kind moments. He'd forgiven her for some mistakes in the past. She recalled his almost tender courtesy at The Tidewater party.

Rearranging fruit on a tray, Charlotte wished she could as easily rearrange her crazy life.

And if given her druthers, she'd rather that she and Dean be friends.

Winnie

Winnie shot a glance at Mimi Beale from the passenger side of her friend's car. Why were they stopping at the Magnolia Harbor Inn? Neither Grace nor Charlotte could go with them on their day trip to Charleston.

"Grace has been so worried about one of their guests," Mimi told Winnie. "Lydia needs to get out more."

Winnie froze. Lydia Walkerton?

"So when I met her at hospitality hour the other night," Mimi continued, "I asked her along on our little trip. You don't mind, do you?" Without waiting for an answer, Mimi bounced out of the car. She walked up to the inn's front door and went inside.

I don't mind, but Lydia might. For the life of her, Winnie couldn't figure out why the woman had gotten so upset over that baby quilt.

Grace hadn't understood why Lydia rushed out of The Busy Bees meeting either. She probably didn't know Mimi—who was everybody's best friend—had invited Lydia to spend the day with her and Winnie.

So much for a getaway. Winnie slapped the door handle. She'd just gotten past that fuss with Patty, and now she might have to deal with another one? Well, she'd let Mimi handle this. Winnie moved to the back seat.

Fanning herself with a hand, she smiled as Mimi and Lydia, not appearing overly pleased, got into the car.

"I'm so glad you could come with us," Winnie said brightly. "I know you'll love the tearoom."

Lydia turned around just enough to be polite. "I'm sure I will," she said stiffly.

Winnie's mind blanked as if Lydia had clicked a remote.

Bubbly Mimi, however, had never met a silence she couldn't fill. She talked about the sights they'd see in Charleston, the tearoom's delicious sandwiches and desserts, and the tea plantation on Wadmalaw Island. "They have a wonderful tea bar where you can sample all the teas they grow. Every time I go, I want to take it all home with me."

Winnie added her two cents here and there.

To her surprise, Lydia loosened up a little, mentioning teahouses she'd visited in Japan when her late husband was in the military.

Soon Mimi was zooming into Charleston's busy outskirts, heading for the city's historic downtown.

After parking the car, they strolled along the waterfront where fresh Atlantic breezes cooled the summer day. Though she'd visited the city a hundred times, Winnie never tired of seeing beautiful old churches and stately eighteenth- and nineteenth-century homes, many with pillars and ornate ironwork, along the palm-lined streets.

"I've traveled in the Far East and Europe," Lydia said. "But I haven't seen much of my own country other than New York. This is a lovely city."

Soon they were browsing the Charleston City Market, one of Winnie's all-time favorite places. Open-air sheds offered everything from furniture to lobster hush puppies. Since they were eating lunch at the tearoom, Winnie skipped the hush puppies. However, she couldn't resist a biscuit with pimento cheese.

"We'll walk it off," Winnie reassured Lydia and Mimi, who had also given in to temptation.

She'd never spoken truer words. After exploring the large market and walking to the tearoom, their stomachs, as well as their feet, craved a break.

The tearoom was the perfect place for it. Cream-colored paneling and arches created an airy backdrop for elegant furniture made of native woods and patterned rugs of cream, rust, and soft blue. Servers in historical costumes showed them to their table.

A little while later, Winnie was savoring okra pilaf—a dish of rice, bacon, okra, onions, and green bell peppers—along with plantation muffins.

Mimi talked Lydia into trying the shrimp-and-cheese grits, and Lydia discovered a new favorite.

"The tea's good here," Winnie whispered to Lydia. "But if I were you, I'd wait until we go to the plantation. The tea there is to die for."

They all ate slices of chocolate-pecan pie with bourbon glaze for dessert.

"We'll walk the pie off too, right?" Lydia sent Winnie a small, sideways smile.

Winnie blinked. Was Lydia making a joke? Chuckling, she shot back, "You can walk all you want. I got my steps in back at the market. When we get to the tea plantation, I'm taking the trolley."

They all laughed.

After lunch, they arrived at the tea plantation and rode the trolley along roads lined with gnarled oaks. With graceful, lacy moss draped on their branches, the trees wore their age well. So did acres of shiny, brilliant tea plants.

By the time they reached the gift shop, Mimi was wiping her damp forehead nonstop. "Sweet tea, here I come. I don't care what kind, as long as it's cold and wet."

Winnie could take the heat—she'd grown up with only one fan

in the house—but she still welcomed the air-conditioning as they entered the gift shop.

"I'm impressed." Lydia glanced around the spacious room. "I don't know if I've ever seen this many varieties of tea in one place."

Mimi made a beeline for a dispenser with Carolina mint sweet tea and filled a glass.

Lydia followed Winnie to the unsweetened peach tea.

"I have to watch my sugar," Winnie explained. She motioned toward Mimi. "Why don't you get some of the best stuff over there?"

Lydia shook her head. "Sorry, but I'm not sure if I'll ever get used to sweet tea. It tastes like syrup to me."

"I suppose it does if you're not used to it," Winnie said with a chuckle.

Two families with several children apiece entered the shop. Most of the kids were well-behaved. But a preschooler turned on a tea spigot at the bidding of his preadolescent brother, who stretched out underneath it and opened his mouth wide.

As their aggravated parents halted the operation and cleaned up the mess, Winnie and Mimi choked back their laughter.

Lydia hardly gave the chaos a glance. She seemed transfixed by a solemn, dark-eyed baby girl sitting in her stroller. Neither of them cracked a smile. They just stared at each other like animals in neighboring zoos.

Winnie and Mimi, wiggling fingers and cooing at the little one, were rewarded with a precious grin.

But Lydia didn't move. She gazed, unblinking, at the child.

Winnie started to edge Lydia away when the baby suddenly started bawling at the top of her lungs. Two toddlers in the group added their screeches as well. Soothing, hushing, and bribing, the parents hurriedly purchased tins of cookies and herded their flock outside again.

Mimi and Winnie greeted their favorite teas like old friends and debated buying new ones.

Lydia's interest in the teas seemed to have vanished. During their discussion about green tea with pomegranate versus rooibos hibiscus herbal tea, she said, "Do you mind if I take a little walk while you shop?"

"Not at all," Winnie answered. "But is that bunch with the kids still out there? If you're searching for peace and quiet, that might not be your best option."

"I saw them take the trolley," Lydia said. "The picnic grounds look quiet and shady."

It didn't seem to bother Lydia that Winnie and Mimi stayed inside. They watched her slowly stroll among the oaks, her sleek, dark head bowed.

"I hope she solves the world's problems while she's out there in the heat." Winnie gulped another swallow of peach tea.

"I hope she at least solves whatever's bothering her." Mimi gestured toward a vacant bench near a window. "Let's take a seat before somebody else grabs it."

As Winnie expected, Mimi wanted to talk. "I think Lydia is upset about a new man in her life."

Winnie shook her head. "She's never mentioned one except her late husband. I wonder if it's about her children, but Lydia has never said one word about kids either."

Mimi agreed, then switched to rehashing the parties at the Magnolia Harbor Inn and The Tidewater, the thefts, and Ian.

"He doesn't seem like a bad man. In fact, he reminds me of some guys I knew in music school—role players, with capes and swords and drama." Mimi chuckled, but she studied Winnie. "He's awfully good-looking, and he seems to adore Grace. Does she like him too?"

"She seems uncomfortable with his attention," Winnie said.

Despite her negative answer, she recalled that her niece had defended Ian a little too often. Surely she didn't prefer that man, who maybe should be in jail, to handsome, helpful Spencer?

Mimi interrupted Winnie's reverie by discussing the inn's other guests. "That young couple is just so cute. They can't take their eyes off each other."

"Young love," Winnie said, smiling.

"Tom and Bonnie are great," Mimi said. "Did you know they used to be art professors? Tom said they taught at a college somewhere in Rhode Island."

Winnie frowned. Grace hadn't mentioned that. "Are you sure? As far as I know, Bonnie hasn't said anything about teaching art."

"I was talking to them at The Tidewater party," Mimi said. "When Tom mentioned teaching art, Bonnie shushed him as if he'd said something terrible."

Why would Bonnie want to keep that a big secret? Winnie puzzled over the woman's strange reaction, finding no answer.

As Winnie and Mimi rose to pay for their purchases, Winnie decided to ask Grace about Tom and Bonnie when she saw her next.

As they waited in line, both Winnie and Mimi noticed Lydia walking in circles around one big tree.

"She's been out there quite a while," Winnie remarked. She considered checking on their companion but hesitated. Even though they were getting along better today, she didn't want to interrupt Lydia's thoughts and take the chance of upsetting her again.

Mimi seemed to read Winnie's mind. "I'll take her another glass of tea."

Watching from a small side window, Winnie saw Mimi intercept Lydia, who accepted the tea. Mimi then joined in Lydia's repetitive stroll. It appeared that Mimi was listening more than talking. Before long, the two women returned, and Lydia headed for the restroom.

"Lydia didn't say much," Mimi confided to Winnie when Lydia was out of earshot. "But she did mention that she'd been struggling with a decision she'd made. Lydia had thought she was right, but now she wonders if she made the biggest mistake of her life."

It wasn't a lot of information, but it explained why Lydia had been so upset. Yet what did that have to do with her strong reaction to Winnie's offer of that little baby quilt?

On the way home, Winnie's mind spun with decisions Lydia could have made and now regretted.

One possibility made her sit up straight. What if that quilt had reminded Lydia of a baby she'd birthed long ago? A baby who'd recently shown up to destroy her well-designed life?

Winnie exhaled. That would explain why Lydia had gotten so mad. And why she'd been so closemouthed about her family.

She shook her head and told herself that maybe she'd been watching too many movies lately.

Winnie studied Lydia, who had a set to her shoulders that she hadn't had before. Winnie heard no smiles in her rare comments, but Lydia didn't droop like an unwatered plant anymore either. Maybe during her walk outside the gift shop, she'd made up her mind about her problems.

Winnie hoped so. Her heart ached for Lydia. She shouldn't be sad and miserable, especially during her vacation.

When they drove up in front of the inn, Grace stuck her head out the front door. At the sight of the three women, she raised her eyebrows.

Winnie almost laughed at Grace's surprised expression.

"You're just in time for hospitality hour," Grace said, recovering quickly. "Charlotte made her mini crab pizzas tonight. You don't want to miss those."

"Why, thank you, honey. I think I will." Winnie didn't mind staying. She'd left last night's fried chicken in the fridge for Gus's supper.

"Thank you," Mimi said. "I'd love to stay. Besides, Doug and the girls will be happy to have an excuse to eat at Aunt Patsy's Porch." She took her phone out of her purse, presumably to call her husband, and headed for the back veranda.

"After that huge lunch, I can't believe I'm hungry, but I am," Lydia marveled, then followed Mimi.

Grace's eyebrows shot up a second time as she leveled an incredulous gaze at her aunt. "What's going on?"

Winnie shrugged.

Grace studied her face but didn't say anything else as she guided Winnie to the veranda, where they joined the others.

Charlotte smiled when she saw her aunt. "I'm so glad you're here."

Winnie gave her a big hug, then stepped back to regard the refreshments table. "As always, everything looks wonderful."

"Thanks." Charlotte poured Winnie a glass of unsweetened tea and handed it to her.

Winnie took a plate and helped herself to the pizza and the fruit salad. She sat down next to Mimi and Lydia, who were telling Grace about their trip to Charleston. Winnie was pleased to see that Lydia was eating more than a few bites of the crab pizza. She couldn't blame her. It was delicious.

The arrival of Tom and Bonnie aroused Winnie's curiosity again. If they were retired art professors, as Mimi had said, why was it such a secret?

The couple greeted everyone warmly, then helped themselves to the food. After Charlotte poured them glasses of wine, they sat down at a table.

As everyone sat eating and enjoying the view of the lake, Bonnie took her knitting out of her bag and set to work.

Lydia glanced over at the hat Bonnie was making. "What a beautiful pattern."

Winnie saw her opening to bring up what was nagging her. "Well, no wonder you and Tom make such beautiful things. I heard you taught art at a college in Rhode Island. Do you paint and draw too?"

Tom froze.

Clicking her tongue, Bonnie shook her head. "I'm afraid someone's greatly exaggerated our talents. I've led a few sessions on knitting and crocheting at a local craft store." She gave a little laugh. "I taught Tom, but neither he nor I ever taught art at a college."

"So what did the two of you do before you retired?" Winnie asked.

"Tom and my brother ran the family business, a tool and die company," Bonnie answered. "And I mostly raised our children."

Bonnie sounded like she was telling the truth, and Winnie would have believed her except Tom stared at his hands, acting like a small boy caught sneaking cookies.

Winnie quickly changed the subject, but it bothered her. It bothered her a lot, and she couldn't say why. She chided herself for being silly. People told little white lies all the time.

But why would someone hide the fact that they taught art at a college? More likely, they'd be proud of their work and want to talk about it.

During the rest of the social hour, Winnie's thoughts scratched at the contradiction as if it were a mosquito bite. She decided to bounce it off Grace and Charlotte later.

After Mimi went home and the guests retired to their suites, Winnie stayed to help her nieces with the cleanup. As they worked, she told them what was on her mind.

Grace stopped washing one of the silver trays and glanced at Charlotte, then turned to Winnie. "There have been some developments."

"What kind of developments?" Winnie asked.

Grace proceeded to tell her about Ian's theft of the museum books. "He also said that he saw Tom put something into his pocket at The Tidewater."

Winnie gasped. "Do you really think Tom stole Dean's clock?"

"I don't," Charlotte chimed in. "Bonnie witnessed Ian lingering near the clocks and then slip something under his cape."

"Who is telling the truth?" Winnie asked.

"That's what we've been trying to figure out," Grace said. She resumed washing the silver tray.

Winnie had been hoping that talking to her nieces would provide her with some answers. But the conversation had raised even more questions.

18

Grace

"Tennis tomorrow?" Grace echoed into the phone. She was sitting on the veranda with Charlotte and Winston after the social hour, trying to relax after such a long day. She certainly hadn't expected an invitation from Spencer this evening.

Winston, who had been snoozing at Grace's feet, pricked up his ears.

Charlotte turned to her sister and whispered, "Spencer?"

Grace nodded.

"I know that August isn't the best weather for tennis," Spencer said. "But if we play in the morning or evening, maybe the court won't fry us like eggs."

Contrary to their last phone conversation, Spencer sounded like his usual easygoing self. Still, Grace's thoughts bounced like straying tennis balls. Had he already heard the news about Ian's museum heist? If he had, did she want to hear him talk about it?

Pushing away the thoughts, she imagined an early morning tennis match. It sounded so nice. Cooler breezes, sunshine . . . and maybe, just maybe, a little fun.

"Yes," Charlotte whispered. "Tell him yes."

"It sounds great," Grace told Spencer. "Evening is out for me, but if you don't mind an early game, would six thirty work?"

"Sure, I can do that. I'll pick you up."

"See you then." Grace disconnected.

"Sounds like you have a date," Charlotte teased.

"It's only tennis," Grace said as she swatted her sister's arm. "Nothing more."

Spencer showed up at the inn at six thirty the next morning. Thankfully, he didn't seem any more inclined to discuss Ian than Grace was.

As soon as they arrived at the tennis court, they jumped right into their match. How great it felt to run and smack the ball.

Spencer was good, making an occasional spectacular shot as they volleyed back and forth. If her ball hadn't hit the line to finish the last set, he might have defeated her.

As it was, Grace gulped a large swallow of satisfaction along with her sports drink. When he accused her of hiding her expertise, she shrugged.

Spencer frowned, but his twinkling eyes spoiled the effect. "You know, if you drag a guy out of bed at the crack of dawn to play, you should at least let him win."

"That's not in the rules," Grace said. "On the other hand, I should be a good sport." She grinned. "All right, I'll only gloat for a month or two."

"Thanks a lot." He laughed. "So, how about a consolation prize?"

"What kind of prize?"

"A free breakfast at your inn. I'll even help clean up." Spencer folded his hands as if pleading for mercy. "Please. Don't you want to rescue me from an ancient bagel and some extremely questionable orange juice?"

"That does sound like a desperate situation," she said. "And Charlotte is making orange-almond buttermilk pancakes this morning."

Spencer smiled. "Then I can come?"

"Of course you can." Grace smiled too. "If you eat them all, I won't be tempted to finish them off tonight."

They continued to banter as they packed up their gear, but Spencer grew a little quieter as they got into his car and set off for the inn.

When an odd note crept into his voice, Grace wondered if she'd said something to offend him. Or had that silly tennis match meant more to him than she thought?

"Is there something on your mind?" she finally prompted.

He hesitated. "Well, yeah. Dean told me that after the theft at his place, he got a little crazy. He blasted Charlotte and you as if it were your fault."

Grace winced. "He certainly did. I chalked it up to his being upset, but I'm afraid Charlotte's still steaming."

Spencer chuckled ruefully. "I think Dean would explain if he thought she'd give him a chance."

"Explain what?"

"His grandfather gave him the clock, which has been in the family for generations," Spencer said. "To make matters worse, it was stolen right around the anniversary of his grandfather's death."

"Oh my." No wonder Dean had blown up. Grief sometimes did that to people. "But why did he wait so long to confront us? The clock was stolen days before he came over to the inn."

"Naturally, Dean was already upset about the theft," Spencer answered. "Then when Ian went back to The Tidewater, Dean completely lost it and took it all out on you and Charlotte."

"I suppose it was a sort of compliment that he felt safe expressing his anger to us," Grace said.

"I was hoping you'd take it that way," he said as he parked in front of the inn. "Dean is really sorry, and he wanted me to approach you.

Maybe you can help me explain to Charlotte."

"So our tennis game was a cover to make Dean's apology for him?" Grace had cooled down from the match, but now she felt her face flush.

"No, it wasn't like that," Spencer insisted. "I've been meaning to ask you to play so you'd get away for a little while. And it was fun, wasn't it?" He grimaced. "Even though you beat me."

Grace couldn't help but laugh.

"I only agreed to help Dean because all this has worn you down," he continued. "I thought if I could smooth things over between Dean and Charlotte, there would be one less battle for you to mediate."

Grace hadn't acknowledged to herself that Charlotte's storms made her own role more difficult. Now, with Spencer's gaze fixed on her, she saw how he might think that resolving the conflict would solve the problem or at least lighten her load. And she had to admit there was some truth in what he was saying.

"Okay, we can try." Grace smiled. "But let's both eat—and make sure Charlotte eats too—before we play diplomat."

"Sounds like a plan." He got out of the car and retrieved her bag from the trunk.

Grace exited the car too. She hadn't expected the small rush of relief that loosened her taut muscles. Still, the idea of approaching Charlotte made her realize how tired she was. Her body, annoyed at this much exertion, informed her in no uncertain terms that fortysomething wasn't nearly the same as twentysomething.

Nevertheless, as she and Spencer walked to the front door, the sun's steady climb into the heavens made her feel as if they could do this. The lake breezes refreshed her like a magic elixir.

Then a cold realization halted her in her tracks.

Ian never skipped breakfast.

Grace closed her eyes. Maybe Spencer, who'd essentially invited himself, planned to confront the historian. To inform Ian that Spencer knew he'd lied about his supposed defense. That would humiliate Ian on so many levels.

"You think I won't play nice with Ian?" Spencer asked, reading her mind.

Grace tried to curb her growing anxiety. "Neither of you appear to be each other's best friend."

"Make that the least of your worries," Spencer urged. "I promise to do my best to keep everybody happy, including Ian."

Perhaps Spencer would confirm Ian's story instead. Grace shook her head at the unlikely notion.

The prospect of a fluffy orange-almond buttermilk pancake helped her gain a little perspective. And when they walked through the door, Winston greeted them. He wagged his tail as Grace petted him.

"I'm going to take a quick shower," Grace told Spencer. "Make yourself at home."

"Winston will keep me company, won't you, boy?" Spencer scratched behind the dog's ears.

Winston leaned into the attention.

After a refreshing shower, Grace thought they might survive this breakfast. She joined Spencer and Charlotte in the dining room, where her sister was putting the finishing touches on the table.

"So here's the tennis champion," Charlotte teased. "Spencer told me all about your match."

"It was close," Grace said.

Spencer put a hand over his heart. "You don't have to pity me," he joked.

They all laughed.

Ian appeared and halted at the door. Spencer greeted him cordially, but Ian only nodded in response. The historian planted himself at the opposite end of the table, gloomily chewing dried cranberries.

If he wanted to isolate himself, so be it. Grace smiled at Spencer to let him know that she didn't expect him to perform social miracles.

As she was pouring coffee, Daniel and Maggie walked in. Grace gave thanks for their arrival. Maybe they would provide a buffer between the two men.

However, the couple seemed tense, and Maggie's red eyes betrayed she'd been crying.

Grace held her breath, wondering if this breakfast would explode after all.

Just in time, Tom and Bonnie strolled into the room and came to the rescue. Unlike the unusually antisocial Ian and the sullen Daniel, Tom readily responded to Spencer's overtures.

More than a twinge of guilt troubled Grace as Bonnie distracted Maggie and reached out to Lydia, who arrived last. How could Grace entertain a shadow of a doubt about the sweet older lady?

Soon Grace's wonder overrode her self-reproach. Lydia, of all people, engaged a sulky Ian with excellent questions about the area's history.

At first, Ian answered in monosyllables, but eventually, his usual enthusiasm shone through his funk. There was no more glowering like a rejected adolescent. After breakfast, he even accompanied Lydia to the veranda, continuing in his signature lecture mode.

When everyone was gone except for Spencer and Charlotte, Grace breathed a sigh of relief. She still didn't understand what Spencer was up to concerning Ian, but at least World War III hadn't broken out during breakfast.

"I'm glad you could join us," Charlotte told Spencer.

He smiled. "Anytime you need someone to eat pancakes, you can always count on me."

"I'll keep that in mind," Charlotte said with a grin.

The inn's phone rang, and Grace answered it. "Magnolia Harbor Inn. How may I help you?"

"This is Jennifer Parker. We met at the party at The Tidewater."

"Oh yes," Grace said, recalling when Dean introduced her to Jennifer and her husband, Chris, who were visiting from Washington, D.C. "What can I do for you?"

"We really enjoyed our time at The Tidewater," Jennifer said. "But I told Chris that when we come back next month, I want to stay at your beautiful mansion."

"We'll be so happy to have you," Grace said.

After Jennifer told her the dates they wanted to book, she asked, "Has either inn recovered the stolen items yet?"

"Unfortunately, no," Grace admitted, hoping Jennifer wouldn't consider it a safety issue.

"I'm sorry to hear that," Jennifer said. "Maybe Chris and I are the jinx."

"What do you mean?" Grace asked.

"First, when we stayed at a B and B in Richmond, Virginia—where I thought we had met the Kleins—a thief took some silver snuffboxes. Then when we came to Magnolia Harbor, your sampler and the clock at The Tidewater disappeared." Jennifer laughed. "I hope you don't think we'll bring you more bad luck."

Grace laughed too. "Of course not." But as she took the reservation, a small wheel began to spin in her mind. Another antique robbery at another bed-and-breakfast? Could it be a coincidence? She thanked Jennifer and hung up.

"Is something wrong?"

Grace jumped. "I'm sorry. I—"

"Almost forgot I was here?" Spencer said with a smile. "I'm deeply insulted."

Grace couldn't say what she was thinking. "That was someone I met at Dean's party, and her talking about it reminded me of his clock." She regretted the words as soon as she said them.

Charlotte narrowed her eyes. "I'd rather we didn't mention Dean or his clock."

Obviously it wasn't the right moment to bring him up. Grace kicked herself for opening her mouth.

"Dean told me he made a fool of himself when he barged in here," Spencer told Charlotte. "He'd like to apologize to you and Grace."

"Right." Charlotte seemed skeptical, but she sounded less venomous. Spencer segued smoothly to Dean's explanation for his behavior.

"It's so hard to lose a grandparent," Charlotte said, her face softening. Spencer nodded. "It's hard to lose anyone you love."

At the sadness in his voice, Grace caught her breath. Spencer rarely referred to his late wife, who had lost her battle with cancer years before. Her own grief at Hank's death, which hadn't surfaced for a while, moistened her eyes.

Charlotte's face softened. "I'm so sorry Dean lost his family's heirloom, especially at the worst time possible. But why didn't he explain?"

"Dean wanted to," Spencer said, "but he was afraid you'd hang up on him."

A faint smile tugged at her lips. "He was probably right."

Grace marveled at the change in her sister. Obviously, Spencer had plenty of experience defusing tense situations.

"Is it okay if I tell Dean he can call you?" Spencer asked.

"Of course." Charlotte smiled, but for a brief moment, her eyes sparked again. "But if he ever shows up at our door, yelling like that again—"

"I'll let you discuss that with him," Spencer interrupted.

The sisters laughed.

But as Grace hugged Charlotte, she could hardly keep back the tears. *What's wrong with me?* She was the one who usually calmed troubled waters and helped emotional guests recover their equilibrium.

Grace offered to finish cleaning up, so Charlotte went home to work on her book. Hopefully, Spencer would also leave so she could collect herself.

Instead, he followed her to the kitchen, poured her a cup of coffee, and insisted she sit down while he loaded the dishwasher.

At his kindness, tears welled up again. Grace grabbed a tissue and dabbed at her eyes. "I must have allergies."

When Spencer didn't comment on the obvious fib, she couldn't stop warm tears from spilling down her face. "Oh, I'm a mess," she blurted and buried her face in her hands.

He paused with a plate in hand. "I don't think you could be a mess if you tried."

Grace shook her head. "You're a bigger liar than I am." She blew her nose, and the sound seemed to echo from the kitchen walls.

Spencer put the plate in the dishwasher and gave her another tissue.

Grace sighed. "Since I'm already a mess, you may as well tell me if you've heard anything about Ian."

He cleared his throat. "I found out his story is completely accurate. In fact, the museum board tried to hire Ian as curator, but he didn't want to leave his college job. He serves as a board member now."

So Ian had told the truth. Grace's instincts had been right.

"I'm sorry I didn't tell you earlier," Spencer said. "You seemed to need a little break more than you needed to hear about my research."

"I did." Grace smiled, despite her sniffles. "It was the best time I've had in ages."

Spencer matched her smile. "Actually, I'd hoped to connect with Ian this morning, maybe set up a time when we could talk. I should have realized that wasn't an option. I should have just told Captain Daley and let him inform Ian, which is what I'm going to do after cleanup." He fixed his eyes on hers. "Now that I've told you."

"I really appreciate your help. I can't imagine why you'd do this for a man who annoys you so much."

Her laid-back friend morphed into the lawman he'd once been. "Ian is innocent until proven guilty. Even if his explanation of this past event seemed irrational, I thought it should be explored."

Grace nodded, impressed with Spencer's integrity.

Forbidding Grace to touch the dishwasher, he finished loading it. Then he poured her another cup of coffee.

"You should eat the last pancake," Grace said.

"My pleasure." As he complied, he made her laugh with stories of the awful meals he ate back at his farm. But his cleanup techniques told Grace he knew his way around a kitchen.

As they said goodbye, Grace thanked him again. "In one morning, you've gotten Charlotte and Dean talking again and reduced the chances that our guest stole from us." She grinned. "Would you care to negotiate world peace next?"

"No thanks." Spencer chuckled. "But if I helped make your day better, then it brightens mine too."

For a moment, Grace was tempted to share the other disturbance rotating in her mind that was left over from her conversation with Jennifer Parker. And this one threatened to grow into an even bigger storm.

At that moment, she spotted Tom and Bonnie ambling toward the lake, arm in arm.

Grace turned back to wave at Spencer as he headed for his car.

She wouldn't breathe a word to anyone about the upsetting thoughts running through her head until she'd done some investigating on her own.

19

Grace

Later that morning, Ian approached Grace in the dining room, where she was straightening up. "Did you tell the police captain why I took those museum books?" he asked without preamble.

Grace raised her chin. "No, I didn't." It was the truth. Spencer had talked to Daley, as he'd promised. "What did the captain say?"

A small smile curved his lips. "That I am no longer required to remain in the area. They'll contact me if necessary."

"How wonderful for you," she said. Even though it wasn't an outright declaration of his innocence, it certainly was a big step toward clearing his name. "So you're leaving soon?" A pang of regret, stronger than Grace would have expected, tightened her throat.

"No."

"You're not?" She felt an equal pang of annoyance.

"That would make me less than what I am." Ian struck a nineteenth-century hero's pose. "I shall stay until the thief is caught and I have been completely exonerated."

"Oh . . . great," Grace said.

When Ian went upstairs to his suite, she escaped to the veranda, taking deep breaths of sultry air. It helped to calm her down, but her muscles tightened at the sight of Tom and Bonnie returning from their walk.

Suddenly a new plan came to her, and she hurried into the kitchen to fetch a pitcher of tea.

Even the dapper couple appeared wilted as they entered the inn. They welcomed Grace's invitation to sit in the living room and cool down.

Grace poured three glasses of iced tea. "I've heard Florida gets even soggier in August, but I can't imagine that."

"It sure does." Tom gulped his tea. "When we stayed in Jacksonville two years ago, I couldn't stand to set foot outside. Savannah's almost as bad. Bonnie's younger sister lives near there. She's only free during summers, so that's when we go." He snorted. "It's like living in a sauna."

Bonnie agreed, then changed the subject by talking about the climate in Rio de Janeiro and Buenos Aires.

As Grace listened, she realized Bonnie had deftly changed the subject like that before. Though always talkative, she didn't elaborate on seeing her sister. Plus, had she ever described their stays in the States? Not that Grace recalled.

"Charlotte and I are hoping to take a break next month." She rattled the ice cubes in her glass. "We thought we'd go to Virginia or maybe even farther north. Can you recommend any B and Bs there?"

"We liked Virginia," Tom answered. "But that time of year, New England is the best—"

"Dear, you're still quite red in the face," Bonnie interrupted. "Are you sure you took your blood pressure medication today?" She fussed over her husband until he agreed to return to their room to check his pillbox. "I think you should rest."

Tom gave Grace a rueful smile. "She'll make me live to be a hundred whether I want to or not."

"Exactly right." Bonnie nodded emphatically. "Thanks for the tea. You're so hospitable. I think you've spoiled us for any inn but yours." Smiling as always, she ushered Tom upstairs.

Bonnie was worried about Tom's blood pressure, yet she wanted him to climb the stairs?

Grace had seen the affectionate glances between them, the way they held hands as they walked. Bonnie really did try to help Tom make healthy food choices. As he said, she appeared to want him to live forever.

Good grief. Grace couldn't begin to think otherwise.

However, underneath their conversation today, she detected nervousness, even tension that seemed to grow until Bonnie had headed Tom off at the pass.

Charlotte had told her about Angel's account of their odd quarrel at the Dragonfly Coffee Shop. Had the couple clashed again?

No, what Grace had sensed was a thin thread of fear woven throughout their chat. What were the Kleins afraid of?

Remembering the places they'd mentioned, Grace headed for her laptop and began a search.

There it was. Confirmation of the so-called jinx robbery Jennifer Parker had mentioned. Grace read the brief newspaper account of the robbery at a bed-and-breakfast in Richmond, Virginia. A collection of antique silver snuffboxes, valued at approximately $4,000, had been taken.

Try as she might, Grace couldn't find any indication that the crime had been solved. Nor could she confirm anything about antique robberies in Jacksonville or Savannah. There were too many crimes and too much information.

And too much conjecture on her part.

She could table her concerns and hope something specific surfaced during conversations. But the small inner alarm that had sounded earlier grew louder by the moment. Ian would certainly proclaim his innocence to the world again. How would the thief—if he or she was still around—react? Could Grace afford to let things ride?

After fiddling with her phone for a few minutes, she called Spencer. If only she didn't have to ask him for another favor.

"Grace, what can I do for you?"

She relaxed a bit. Spencer sounded pleased to hear from her. "I've been doing a little research, hoping to come up with something that might help catch our thief."

"Not a bad idea. Sometimes a seemingly minor detail can prove the most important."

She plunged ahead. "I wondered if you might be able to find out anything about other antique robberies last summer. Thefts in bed-and-breakfasts in Jacksonville, Florida, and Savannah, Georgia."

Thankfully, Spencer didn't ask if she'd closed her eyes and picked the cities on a map. "You think they might have something to do with yours and Dean's?"

"Maybe. I'm questioning if they might be part of a pattern. It's just an idea," Grace added hastily. She didn't want to even hint at a link to Tom and Bonnie.

He didn't probe further. "So, what have you found so far?"

First, she told him about the theft of antique snuffboxes in Richmond. "I've been doing your basic amateur Internet search, and I tried to check public records. They're overwhelming. I might die of old age before anything makes sense."

"I have a connection or two in those areas," Spencer said. "I'll be glad to dig a little. Anything else?"

"Anything you think would help." Specifying New England would be a bit much. Besides, Grace wanted to explore Tom and Bonnie's alleged connection to a Rhode Island college before pulling Spencer into that scenario. Maybe she'd even find something concrete.

"I'll see what I can find."

After thanking him, Grace disconnected.

She hadn't forgotten about Lydia's odd, lakeside rendezvous with the burly young man. For a change of Internet scenery, Grace decided to explore Lydia's history before tackling Tom and Bonnie's again.

The remainder of Grace's afternoon mostly confirmed that Lydia had not clashed with the law since her teen years. No business scandals and no hints of misconduct of any kind surfaced. Most of the findings centered around Lydia's late husband's distinguished military career and her accomplishments in fashion and large contributions to charity. Lydia restricted her social media to business matters.

Hospitality hour beckoned, so Grace had to shut down her online inquiries. If only she could shut down her mind as easily.

Grace found Charlotte in the kitchen, arranging platters of California rolls, miso soup, and pickled vegetables. "Everything looks great."

Her sister glanced up. "Thanks. I'm almost finished."

Grace took plates, napkins, and utensils out to the veranda, and Charlotte transported the platters and drinks.

They had just finished setting up when Tom and Bonnie arrived.

A few minutes later, Grace was surprised to see Lydia join the group.

Bonnie talked to everyone in her usual friendly way. Grace noticed she didn't allow Tom to wander off without her. Was Bonnie still concerned for his health? Or did she fear he might open his mouth once too often? Grace stayed close to the couple, mentally recording everything they said, but nothing seemed significant.

Lydia puzzled Grace almost as much as the Kleins. Though quiet, she appeared more social than before her Charleston trip. Pain remained visible on her face, but the thunderstorm that had darkened her eyes seemed to have calmed. To Grace's relief, she ate a small plateful of sushi.

When Grace asked if she'd seen any more local sights, Lydia said, "Well, I visited your town's hospital today."

"Are you all right?" Grace asked, concerned.

"I'm fine," Lydia answered. She didn't elaborate.

Grace didn't want to pry into her guest's personal business, so she didn't ask any more questions. Instead, she excused herself to help

Charlotte collect empty plates and bring more California rolls from the kitchen.

Maybe the food service interlude would give her a minute to make sense of the contradictions pinging off the walls in her mind. Bonnie was so thoughtful. How could Grace even think she was capable of anything nefarious?

And had Lydia been wrestling with a major health problem? If so, no wonder she'd experienced trouble eating and sleeping. But why would she come from New York City, with so many famous specialists, to Magnolia Harbor and its small hospital? Did she just need some time away from the bustle of the city?

The huge young man with whom she'd quarreled seemed the picture of health. Maybe too vigorous . . .

"Earth to Grace." Charlotte tapped her on the shoulder. "Where are you this evening?"

"Inside my own head, I guess."

Charlotte set her tray of sushi on the counter. "What's going on? I know I've buried myself in working on my book the past few days, but I haven't noticed any major changes around here."

At the sound of footsteps in the hallway, a genuine smile blossomed on Charlotte's face. "Well, maybe one."

"Hey." Dean breezed in, smiling. "Hope you don't mind my invading your kitchen, but I'll be glad to assist if I can."

Grace winced. *No recipes, please.*

Charlotte's smile didn't dim. She thanked Dean and handed him her tray, which he carried to the veranda.

"Friends again," Charlotte said cheerfully. She retrieved a fresh tray of pickled veggies from the fridge and left the kitchen.

Grace stood for a moment, attempting to regroup. So, the truce Spencer had negotiated was in full force. He'd been right—the burden of their fight had disappeared from Grace's backpack of troubles. A few more might drop if she shared them with her sister. Maybe after social hour, they could sit on the porch swing and talk.

When Grace returned to the veranda with a pitcher of water, Ian appeared. He wore a scarlet cape, a gold beret, and a determined expression. *He may as well sound a trumpet.* Proclamation time had arrived.

"Friends—for it is my hope that some of you consider me a friend—I come to you this evening to unseal my lips and share my heart."

His audience showed no signs they heard him. However, no one left.

Apparently, this reaction encouraged the historian, and he launched into a detailed defense of his earlier theft and rescue of the books from the museum, including the years of publication and summaries of their content. Ian finally described the museum board president's support and his own acquittal.

Charlotte stared, and Grace realized she hadn't yet told her of Spencer's findings. They definitely needed to touch base.

"Perhaps you had already decided I would never have taken well-preserved artifacts from these excellent innkeepers." Ian gestured toward Grace and Charlotte, then Dean. "I hope so. But if not, it is my fervent desire that you would accept the police captain's conclusion that I am no more a suspect in these thefts than any of you."

Alarms sounded in Grace again. She glanced at Tom and Bonnie. There was no reaction from them.

Grace was so caught up in her own thoughts that she was unable to absorb the rest of Ian's speech. The others still engaged him as briefly as possible, but they did shake his hand. Smiling, she did likewise, but she cut him short by saying she needed to speak to Charlotte.

"You and Dean have plenty to talk about, I imagine," Grace whispered to her sister. "I'll clean up."

"Thanks." With a slight nod toward Ian, Charlotte whispered,

"I'm still not absolutely certain about him. If he asks you out, think about it before you say yes, okay?"

Grace rolled her eyes.

Thank goodness some of Ian's historical friends showed up. Grace could excuse herself from his invitation to join in their evening by pleading kitchen duty.

Afterward, she returned to her laptop, checking websites of Rhode Island colleges and their faculty.

Her phone rang. Spencer. Had he learned something?

"I confirmed the theft of snuffboxes at the bed-and-breakfast in Richmond—exactly as you described," he said. "The police there suspected a relative of the inn's owner, but that didn't pan out."

Grace tensed and remained silent, not trusting herself to speak.

"I don't know where you got your information about Jacksonville and Savannah," Spencer went on. "But you were right about them too. One year ago, a gold coin disappeared from an inn in Savannah. Two years ago, a small nineteenth-century painting was stolen from a bed-and-breakfast in Jacksonville."

Her pulse quickened, and a lump of dread dropped into her stomach. *Please let me be wrong.*

"That's not all," Spencer said. "All three incidents are part of a decade-long pattern of antique thefts on the East Coast of small articles that can be easily concealed. They're valuable but usually not so valuable they create an international splash, which would make them difficult to sell. The thief never takes more than one every six months to a year, letting any uproar die down. Cautious type. Smart."

"If it's the same thief, then why did he take two items here?" Grace asked.

"He got greedy, I guess. It happens."

"Thank you. I know this will be useful." What else could Grace say? With only circumstantial evidence, she couldn't implicate Tom and Bonnie.

"Well, I thought you'd want to know." Spencer paused. "And I thought you needed to know something else."

His hesitation didn't bode good news. She took a deep breath. "Tell me."

"While I was digging, I also did an unofficial background check on your other guests." Spencer repeated what Grace already knew about Lydia. "No problem there, I'm sure. But I also connected with a detective friend of mine who works with the police department in Austin, Texas."

"But Captain Daley found only a couple of underage drinking charges against Daniel and Maggie. Nothing else."

"Sure, nothing official. But according to my friend, Magdalena Gutiérrez had a bad habit of stealing expensive articles when she was a teenager."

No. Grace's brain reeled. *Not Maggie.*

"Her father talked the victims out of prosecuting her and used his influence to hush up any whispers about the thefts," Spencer explained. "I'm so sorry to upset you."

She fumbled for words. "I-I appreciate your thoroughness."

"I was hoping to clear things up for you," he said gently, "but it's better that you're aware of what you're dealing with." His voice sharpened. "Be sure to tell me if anything else surfaces. In all the other theft cases, firearms were not involved and no one got hurt. But you never know."

"I'll be fine." Grace hadn't wanted to think about that possibility, but creaks in the nighttime inn's quiet wouldn't let her forget.

"Seriously. In fact, I'll plan to check around your place tonight."

"Oh, you don't need to do that."

"I'll be there around two to make sure everything's fine." Spencer hung up before she could respond.

Grace didn't know whether to be mad or glad. She rubbed her aching temple. If only she could go to bed and forget about the thefts, but she knew her tangled thoughts would keep her awake until the wee hours. She'd probably be up to offer Spencer some tea when he checked the place out at two.

When she tried to continue her search regarding Tom and Bonnie, she was unable to type a word. She couldn't stop contemplating the new information about Maggie.

The young woman was from a wealthy family and obviously didn't need money. So why had she taken to stealing? To rebel against her controlling father?

Grace had assumed John Paul Gutiérrez had demanded Daniel and Maggie return simply because he couldn't bear their independence. But perhaps he'd heard of the thefts at the inns and feared his daughter would be arrested. Maybe he'd tried to bring her home under his protection once again.

Grace didn't know how long she wrestled with her notions and emotions. Eventually, one realization made her gasp. She hadn't seen Daniel and Maggie since breakfast.

It wasn't like them to stay away from the inn for so long, and it certainly wasn't like Daniel to miss hospitality hour.

She recalled the couple's tension and Maggie's red eyes at breakfast. Had the young woman given in to that thieving impulse again? Perhaps she was trying to talk Daniel into returning to Texas.

Grace hurried to the upstairs veranda, where she could view the inn's grounds in every direction. No sign of their car. Perhaps they'd simply gone out for the day and evening.

At least that was what Grace told herself.

But something made her knock on their door. Then call to them. Then turn her master key in the lock.

The Dogwood Suite was as lovely as when Grace had first prepared it for Daniel and Maggie.

But their clothes, suitcases, and personal effects were gone.

20

Grace

Early the next morning, Grace found Charlotte in the kitchen. She told her sister about Maggie's criminal past and the newlyweds' abrupt departure.

"I can't believe that Maggie was a thief," Charlotte said. "And why would they leave now? Their suite is paid through the weekend, isn't it?"

"Yes, but maybe they've returned to Texas early after all."

"Wild horses couldn't drag Daniel back there before he was good and ready," Charlotte said. "I don't think Maggie wanted to go either."

"Then where did they go?" Grace asked.

"Her father said they had no money, but that doesn't mean they were broke," Charlotte suggested, raising a knowing eyebrow.

"That isn't very reassuring." Grace tried not to think about Maggie's possible stash, hidden for years from her father's penetrating eyes. "Maybe they simply panicked. With first one theft here, then another, Daniel was afraid the police would find out about Maggie's past and arrest her, even if she was innocent. So they left."

"I hope you're right."

"I think I am," Grace answered. "After all, Spencer didn't mention any thefts during Maggie's college years."

"Did you tell Captain Daley?" Charlotte asked.

"Not yet," Grace said, knowing she'd only been delaying the inevitable. The captain had instructed them to notify him of any changes in their guests' plans and any details that might be of interest in the case. "It's still quite early, so I'm going to check on a few things first."

She wanted to do more research on the nagging questions about Rhode Island colleges and art faculty members before talking to Daley.

"Sounds good," Charlotte said as she set to work preparing breakfast.

Grace returned to her private quarters. Winston settled in beside her when she opened her laptop. Perhaps exploring facts would make her staggering brain cells line up again.

She absently petted the dog as she searched faculty directories of several universities. When she didn't find any Kleins, she focused on various art departments.

While scrolling through one of the college's alumni magazines, an archive photograph materialized on her screen.

Grace sucked in her breath. Tom and Bonnie Klein, looking a decade younger, gazed back at her.

When she read the caption, she sat back. It said the school was hosting a retirement celebration for art professors Raymond and Marge Callahan.

In answer to Grace's text, Charlotte poked her head inside her sister's quarters. "The scones for breakfast are in the oven, and everything else is nearly ready. What did you want to tell me?"

Grace closed the door behind her, then pulled up the photo she'd found. "Look at this."

Charlotte dropped onto the sofa. "Wow, that's Tom and Bonnie. They looked great back then."

Grace folded her arms. "Read the caption."

"But they have to be the Kleins," Charlotte insisted. "Why would they change their names?"

"It appears they had some very good reasons." Even after the shock had worn off, Grace didn't want to say what she suspected. But she forced herself to outline what she and Spencer had discovered.

Charlotte hugged Winston. "You think those sweet old people stole from us and Dean? And from other B and B owners?"

"After finding out about Maggie, I'm not sure about anything right now," Grace admitted. "But there are several problems concerning Tom and Bonnie that I can't explain away."

"What do you mean?"

Grace rubbed her temples, trying to loosen the iron band that now tightened around her head. "Not only did they lie about their names, but when Winnie mentioned that they'd taught art at a college in Rhode Island, Bonnie denied it."

"Maybe they're famous," Charlotte suggested. "They might be guarding their privacy."

"I don't think so. I've found several past references to their judging juried art shows and teaching occasional seminars. Still, they're not exactly household names."

"Perhaps they're trying to hide from undesirable relatives or enemies of some kind."

"That's possible, I suppose." Grace bit her lip. "If they were indeed in Richmond at a bed-and-breakfast—Jennifer Parker was accurate about every detail of that robbery—then that makes me wonder. A lot."

"*If* they were there," Charlotte said.

"I don't want this to be true any more than you do." Grace's voice trembled. "That's why I'm going to settle it once and for all. When I call Captain Daley about Daniel and Maggie, I'll also tell him about Jennifer's phone call and send him this picture."

"You're hoping he'll check with the Richmond people?" Charlotte asked.

"Exactly. Then it will be up to him." Maybe that would diminish the throbbing that now pounded her head like a drum.

Charlotte handed Winston to Grace, and the dog pressed his fluffy head against her cheek.

For a moment, neither said anything while Winston worked his comforting magic.

Reluctantly, Grace broke his spell. "There are other things that make me suspect Tom and Bonnie."

"What other things?"

"Tom's burn, for instance. For an elderly man, he recovered remarkably well from a nasty injury." Grace sighed. "Ian told me he saw Tom pocket something at Dean's party, using his injured hand with a lot more dexterity than he expected. With that bandage, he'd leave no fingerprints."

"A fake burn?" Charlotte blinked. "You never told me that."

"I didn't want to plant unfounded ideas in your mind." Plus, Grace doubted that her sister would have believed Ian.

"What other red flags made you suspect them?"

"The way Bonnie interrupted Tom when he mentioned their domestic travels. Again, it was as if she were covering up their past. It wouldn't be noticeable unless you knew about the antique robberies that had taken place at the other B and Bs."

"But if Tom and Bonnie are behind this whole mess, why steal two items in Magnolia Harbor?" Charlotte asked. "Especially since the second one wasn't nearly as valuable."

"Spencer thought maybe they were getting greedy," Grace replied. "But they would have risked less if they simply took one of greater value."

Charlotte sat up straight. "Perhaps they hadn't planned to take Dean's clock. You know how Tom loves his pocket watch and our grandfather clock. Maybe he couldn't resist pulling off his own personal heist." She paused. "You know, I'll bet that's what they were fighting about at the Dragonfly."

For a moment, Grace petted Winston's head in silence. If only all humans were as loving and trustworthy as their dog. "First, Ian and his brouhaha. Then Maggie. Now Tom and Bonnie may have stolen not only from us but from other innkeepers." *What about Lydia and that angry young man?* She gritted her teeth, refusing to go there. "I hate all this."

"Me too." Charlotte enclosed Grace and Winston in a big hug. "Maybe Captain Daley will find out that Maggie is innocent, Jennifer is mistaken, and there's a really good explanation for Tom and Bonnie lying about their background. One that has nothing to do with stealing."

"That would be great," Grace said. Charlotte's optimism often lifted Grace's spirits, but this morning, it put only a small dent in her dread. She pulled out her phone and dialed the police station.

Grace's conversation with Captain Daley was brief. He invited her to send him the photo at the college retirement party, agreed to follow up with the bed-and-breakfast in Richmond, and promised to let her know about the identity question.

No urgency colored his level voice. Had the captain merely added her concern to the bottom of his to-do list?

"I'm not sure if Daley realizes this is important," Grace told her sister.

"Stop worrying," Charlotte said. "He always stays calm, and it's not as if you handed him definite proof. He'll call when he has something solid to tell us. For now, let's do what we always do. Serve breakfast and keep our guests happy."

Grace nodded. Summoning every hostess instinct that she possessed, she served the meal with as much normalcy as she could muster.

In her years of co-owning the inn, she'd handled plenty of tense situations. Couples who had brought far more baggage than the suitcases they hauled up the stairs. Cranky old ladies who wanted eggs over impossible and toast points, not slices, thank you. After Grace had pampered them, most mellowed and eventually related well to others.

An outsider would say this morning was no exception. Since Ian's vindication, breakfast had morphed from a minefield to a pleasant meadow. This morning, conversations bloomed like flowers under a sunny sky.

Grace hoped the facade would last. She often ducked into the kitchen, checking to see if she'd missed a call from the captain.

So far, nothing.

Tom and Bonnie showered Charlotte with praise for her scrambled eggs and blueberry scones.

"Such a shame we have to leave tomorrow." Bonnie clicked her tongue. "Tom, how will we survive without our favorite chef and our favorite hostess?"

"Oh, I thought you were staying through the weekend." Though her stomach dropped at the news they were leaving so soon, Grace tried to give Bonnie a warm smile.

"I'm sorry to hear it," Charlotte said. She glanced at Grace before slipping out of the room.

Ian looked across the table at Tom. "I've noticed you have been using your hand as if fully healed. Will you be able to remove the bandage soon?"

Grace almost choked.

Tom halted with his fork halfway to his mouth.

"Tom has a high pain threshold," Bonnie said smoothly. "He never complains and hates to be a bother."

"We're so glad you're feeling better, Tom," Grace said, then hastened to change the subject. "Since you're leaving tomorrow, we would love to fix your favorite breakfast. What would you like?"

Tom brightened, and he gave several suggestions.

Grace readily agreed to them all. If Tom anticipated the breakfast of his dreams, then Bonnie might not be able to persuade him to leave. At least not before tomorrow. Surely by then, the captain would call. If only she could retain the Kleins at the inn today, where she and Charlotte could keep an eye on them. An idea popped into her head.

"This afternoon's forecast calls for extreme heat and humidity with possible thunderstorms," Grace said. "Since it sounds like a great day to stay inside, how about holding a poker tournament here? I could see if Winnie and Gus and Spencer would like to join us too."

"What a splendid idea," Ian said.

"I want to do some shopping downtown before the rain," Lydia said. "But I'll be back by one."

"We'll stay close to home this afternoon," Bonnie said. "After enjoying this feast of a breakfast, we really must get our steps in this morning." She turned to Tom. "Are you ready?"

He nodded.

Grace tried not to stare after the Kleins as they left the inn. At least they didn't take their car. They must be planning to return.

Unless they'd lined up a ride elsewhere. Or a chartered jet at the regional airport. If they'd gotten away with stealing for so long, did they need luggage or their present car? She hoped they didn't sense that someone had seen through their charade.

Shaking her head at her absurd imaginings, Grace hurried to the kitchen. She told Charlotte about the poker plan and Tom's requests for breakfast tomorrow.

"I'll make a list." Charlotte grabbed a piece of paper and a pen and started jotting down ingredients.

Ian entered the kitchen. "May I help you with the dishes? I shall also be glad to assist you in any preparations for the poker tournament."

"Thanks for the kind offer, but we wouldn't want to interfere with your time." Grace appreciated his genuine desire to help, but he would linger all morning. How could she and Charlotte talk? Besides, Grace couldn't shake a growing uneasiness about Tom and Bonnie.

"Please allow me to do something," he insisted. "I'm planning to go downtown. Is there anything I can pick up for you while I'm there?"

"That would be wonderful. I have a grocery list right here." Charlotte handed the paper to Ian and gave him directions to Hanson's Farm Fresh Foods. "Thank you."

"It will be my pleasure," he said and left.

When he was gone, Grace drew a sigh of relief.

Charlotte immediately went to work stacking plates, then opened the dishwasher.

But Grace held up a hand. "Let's not wash the dishes this morning."

Her sister wrinkled her nose. "Why not?"

"If Captain Daley confirms something about the Kleins, he'll need their fingerprints. And if they are guilty, they've probably wiped their rooms clean." Grace hesitated. "Tom and Bonnie may be long gone by the time Daley nails something down. My gut feeling tells me they're planning to leave today, not tomorrow."

Charlotte studied her sister. "You've been hanging out with Spencer too much lately."

"Perhaps it's just my overactive imagination. Still, I think I'll go downtown and 'accidentally' run into them. If I'm simply being paranoid, no problem. But if they are trying to pull something, they'll find it harder to connect with their ride or whatever."

"No, *we* will go downtown." Charlotte crossed her arms. "No way am I letting you go by yourself."

"Fine," Grace said, but she was secretly thankful for her company. She grabbed her purse. "Come on. Let's hurry."

Winston ran in circles and yipped.

"Sorry, but you can't go with us." Grace gave him a dog biscuit. "We'll be back soon."

Grace and Charlotte left the inn and jumped into Grace's car. As Grace drove along Lake Haven Road, she told herself what they were doing was crazy. Were they really trying to keep Tom and Bonnie from skipping town so they could be sent to jail?

Images of the couple flooded Grace's mind. Tom and Bonnie knitting hats, socks, and baby sweaters for homeless shelters and pregnancy care centers. Tom demonstrating his golf swing at hospitality hour. Bonnie making others feel at home wherever she went.

Grace dabbed at wetness gathering in the corner of her eye.

"Stop that!" Despite her sharp tone, Charlotte sounded teary too.

"You're right." Grace tightened her jaw. If Tom and Bonnie were stealing, she and Charlotte could help keep them from victimizing others.

Grace found a parking spot, and they exited the car. "Did you hear them say where they were going? I guess they could have made that up as well."

Charlotte shook her head. "At least downtown isn't very big. It shouldn't take too long to find them if they're here."

Given that assumption, what if they encountered Ian before they found Tom and Bonnie? In an emergency, his strength might come in handy. But subtlety wasn't his strong suit. After a few words from him, the Kleins—or whatever their names were—would most likely vanish.

Grace veered in the opposite direction. "Let's stay away from Hanson's."

Charlotte understood perfectly. "We don't need Ian right now."

As they walked down the street, Grace pasted a smile on her face.

"You look absolutely grim. We're supposed to be on a nice morning walk and casually run into them."

"I was never very good at faking nice." Nevertheless, Charlotte shifted the corners of her straight-lipped mouth.

They greeted a couple of acquaintances and chatted briefly.

"It's a shame we can't split up," Grace said when they were alone again, "but I don't think that would be wise."

They wandered down Main Street, pausing occasionally to peer into store windows.

When they ducked inside the Dragonfly Coffee Shop, they asked Angel if she'd seen Tom and Bonnie.

She nodded. "They stopped in about fifteen minutes ago. They seemed to be in a hurry because they took their coffees to go." Angel scanned their faces. "Can't you call them?"

"Actually, no," Charlotte responded. "And right now, we can't explain."

"Did they mention where they were going?" Grace asked.

Angel seemed troubled. "They were arguing. Something about the library."

"Thanks," Charlotte said. "If they show up again, please call me. And don't tell them we asked about them."

They charged out the door.

"We have to slow down," Grace said, forcing herself to stroll. "We can't give them any hint that we're after them."

"I know." Charlotte matched her sister's pace and grimaced. "If we do catch up with them, what should we say?"

"I'm not sure. We'll think of something."

Charlotte halted. "Think quick because there they are."

21

Grace

Tom and Bonnie sat on a bench near the Heritage Library.

Grace's mind blanked like a broken screen. *Focus. We can do this.*

"Tom! Bonnie!" She waved and smiled at them as if she hadn't seen them in ages. She crossed the street with Charlotte, who echoed her greeting.

The Kleins stood as if eager to go.

"My, both of you are downtown," Bonnie remarked. She wore her usual welcoming smile, but she narrowed her eyes.

Tom grinned at them but stood slightly behind his wife as if she were a shield.

"Yes, we decided to take a walk together," Grace said. "I see you've discovered our library. It was a very special place when I was growing up, and it still is."

"You always were a bookworm," Charlotte teased, but her eyes didn't reflect her grin.

"And proud of it," Grace retorted, then turned back to Tom and Bonnie. "I'll bet you'd love to meet our head librarian, Phyllis Gendel. She's such a wonderful person. We've told her that you're two of our favorite guests." She attempted to guide the couple toward the door.

Bonnie didn't move. "I'm sure she's delightful, but Tom and I have business to take care of before we leave tomorrow."

"Can we help?" Charlotte sounded like a Girl Scout. A nervous one.

"No thank you," Bonnie answered. "We can manage everything."

Grace copied Bonnie's sudden veer to the right, matching the woman's surprising quickness. "It's such a lovely morning," she said sweetly. "Perfect for a pleasant walk with friends."

"I need to get my steps in too." Charlotte attached herself to Bonnie's other side.

Silently Tom trailed them like an afterthought.

"Do you know when Magnolia Harbor was first settled?" Grace reviewed the town's history and pointed out older buildings with details that would have made Ian proud. *I sound like a rambling cockatoo.*

Charlotte's sideways glance confirmed that Grace was chattering too much, but she didn't interrupt because she seemed tongue-tied.

Better that her sister say nothing than betray their surveillance. Grace continued the impromptu historical tour, pausing occasionally to greet friends and introduce their guests.

In response, Bonnie nodded and commented like a pleasant robot, but as they continued, she didn't indicate their destination or the urgent business she'd mentioned earlier. Still smiling, she scanned the streets and sidewalks.

Grace wondered what—or whom—the woman expected to see. How long would this thin veneer of a walk with friends last? Grace attempted to steer them toward the block where the police station was located.

But Bonnie looped them back toward the library. Perhaps a tardy cabdriver waited near there. Or an accomplice.

Or would this entire scenario prove to be an example of Grace's ridiculous imaginings?

Her phone rang, and she startled.

"Goodness, we're a bit jumpy today, aren't we?" Bonnie asked, sounding concerned.

Grace removed her phone from her purse and glanced at its screen. Captain Daley.

She slapped the phone to her ear. "Hello?" Grace infused all the cheerfulness she could into her voice. "Well, what are you doing this morning? Charlotte and I decided to walk to the library—"

The barrel of a small pistol probed Grace's side.

Still smiling, Bonnie shook her head ever so slightly. She gestured with a finger for them to keep moving.

Stomach lurching, Grace obeyed.

Charlotte walked as if in a dream—or a nightmare. All the color had drained from her face.

"We tracked the Simses to Atlanta, where he has relatives," the captain said. "The police there are talking to them. As for the Kleins, the owner of the bed-and-breakfast in Richmond identified them from the picture you sent me. He said they called themselves Martin and Linda Church, and they stayed there at the same time the snuffboxes were stolen."

"Do tell," Grace said brightly. Words swam in her mind as if underwater. She couldn't catch them.

"Are you all right?" Daley asked.

"Oh, I'm a little tired. It's been—"

The barrel of the pistol jabbed her.

"Busy, you know." Grace searched desperately for a code word that would rescue them. "But we've had so much fun with our guests lately."

"Hang up," Bonnie hissed.

"Talk to you later," Grace said and disconnected.

Bonnie snatched Grace's phone and slid it into her tote bag, then turned to Charlotte. "Yours too."

Charlotte handed her phone to Bonnie.

"Okay, let's keep smiling," Bonnie said. "We're going to take a nice ride together."

"This isn't right," Tom sputtered.

"Be quiet, Tom." Bonnie's voice hadn't changed one iota. "I told you from the beginning that we must do whatever is necessary to maintain the business. I've always lived life on my own terms, and I don't plan to change now."

Grace tried to repress a shiver. What kind of business would make Bonnie turn violent?

Would the captain understand the hints Grace had dropped?

She attempted to thaw her frozen brain and consider solutions. Instead, her mind turned on her. Why had she brought Charlotte along on this reckless adventure? Why hadn't she asked Spencer instead? Where were the friends and neighbors who always wanted to chat?

If only Ian would materialize. Grace almost groaned. If she actually wanted the historian, he would never show up.

Think. So far, no sign of the police. Grace peered at their captors, then raised her eyebrows at Charlotte. Couldn't the two of them overpower this elderly Bonnie and Clyde?

Her sister apparently didn't want to risk it. She shook her head almost imperceptibly.

Almost.

"Now, ladies, if you're thinking of attacking this old woman, please don't." Bonnie's casual tone burned into Grace. "I'll shoot without thinking twice."

"Don't talk like that," Tom said plaintively. His shoulders stooped, and he suddenly looked like a very old man. "What if the police catch us? What if they shoot back?"

"Listen to him, Bonnie," Charlotte pleaded.

"Be quiet," Bonnie ordered. No light sparkled in her eyes.

Grace shuddered.

As Bonnie faced Tom, she morphed back into her motherly

persona. "Dear, you mustn't upset yourself." She sounded as if she were coaxing him to take his pills. "Look. I see Bob's van over on that side street."

"Bob will help us," Tom said.

Grace couldn't see the driver. One more captor, even if elderly, might make an escape impossible. They must avoid entering the van at all costs.

As they walked, Charlotte had hardly taken her eyes from Grace.

Now, still feeling the gun in her ribs, Grace wiggled a finger at her sister. *Run, Charlotte.* Grace tried to beg with her eyes, the way she'd begged little Charlotte to leave her and her teen boyfriend in peace.

It didn't work then, and it didn't work now. Charlotte set her jaw.

No, Charlotte was going to stick with Grace until the end.

The end. Grace blanched. Was this the end? She'd never expected it to happen at the hands of an elderly woman who had been one of her favorite guests.

Nor would she expect it now.

Warmth surged through Grace as she murmured a prayer. Somehow she and Charlotte would handle this.

She should get Bonnie talking. Surely, under that hard shell, a vestige of the kind woman still lived and breathed. "Bonnie, you know you'll be caught sooner or later," she said gently.

Bonnie's scornful expression constricted her throat.

Still, Grace pushed the words out. "Do you want Tom to go to jail too?"

"Jail?" Tom repeated. "You promised I wouldn't, Bonnie. You promised."

"I always keep my promises," Bonnie assured him. She didn't break stride. "I said I would take care of everything, and I will."

"Okay, okay," he said, his voice trembling.

Grace's heart sank to her ankles. Bonnie didn't just lead Tom around by the nose. She owned him.

A silhouette flattened against a building half a block away. Grace caught her breath. The person looked too tall for the captain, but something about him was familiar. Could it be Spencer?

"Where will you take us?" Grace asked. "I've always wanted to go to Rio."

Charlotte's glare said, *What is the matter with you?*

Bonnie chuckled. Not a nice laugh. "Who knows? You might drift in that direction. Eventually."

The shadow didn't move again. Had Grace imagined it?

When they reached the van, the door slid open. An older man peeked out and grinned at them.

Bonnie glared at Grace and Charlotte and gestured to the door. "Get in."

Grace didn't budge.

Charlotte's expression begged her to cooperate.

"Remember, I will do anything to protect our business," Bonnie said. "Anything."

"I haven't forgotten." Grace lowered her eyes, then sneaked a glance toward the building where she'd last spied their potential phantom rescuer. No movement—

From the opposite direction, someone slammed into Bonnie. She let out a grunt and fell to the pavement with the rescuer. The gun clattered into the street.

Tom wailed.

Grace stumbled, then scrambled for Bonnie's gun at the same time Charlotte did.

A second later, Spencer charged into the melee. He reached the weapon first and held it over Bonnie.

Bob peeled out in the van, but Captain Daley appeared and trained his gun on him. The van screeched to a halt. Lieutenant Wesley Townsend and Officer Greg Warshaw, guns drawn, backed up their captain.

Recovering from her shock, Grace automatically extended a hand to help Bonnie. She halted midway and reached instead for the first rescuer who had crashed into their captor.

Lydia.

Charlotte

Charlotte hardly recognized Spencer and Captain Daley. Their eyes glinted, and they spoke through gritted teeth.

Lieutenant Townsend handcuffed Bonnie and Bob. After Officer Warshaw handcuffed Tom, he tried to calm him down, but the old man alternately wept and swore at him.

Charlotte shook her head, then turned to her sister.

Grace remained silent as she stared at Lydia.

Charlotte was on the verge of both laughter and tears, and she had to say something. "Lydia Walkerton, where did you learn how to tackle?"

She shrugged. "My husband and I lived in difficult places. He was often gone for months at a time, so he insisted I learn self-defense."

"How did you find us?" Charlotte asked.

"I'd just left the Dragonfly when I saw the Kleins escorting you and Grace to the van," Lydia explained. "Bonnie and Grace moved as if glued together. I thought it was odd. Though both you and your sister were smiling, something seemed wrong."

"You were right about that," Charlotte said, pushing back her hair with trembling fingers.

"Then sunlight glinted off something metal in Bonnie's hand." Lydia's pale cheeks reddened. "I didn't stop to ask questions."

"I'm so glad you didn't." Charlotte threw caution to the wind and hugged her.

"Thank you." Grace, who had summoned a shaky smile, finally

spoke up. "If not for you, we might have been on our way to Rio." She shivered. "Floating without a boat."

"We would never have hurt you," Bonnie insisted in a reasonable tone. "That's not our style."

After holding her sister at gunpoint and threatening their lives, she was trying to con them again? Charlotte snarled and clenched her fists.

Grace gripped Charlotte's arm. "Don't listen to her."

"Your sister's right," Spencer said.

Charlotte turned to him. She'd almost forgotten he was there.

Captain Daley dispersed the curious bystanders. "We'll talk to you ladies later," he told Charlotte and Grace. "Go home and get some rest." Then he led Bonnie away, his officers taking charge of Tom and Bob.

Grace cast a longing glance in the inn's direction, but she sank to the ground. Spencer knelt down beside her.

"They left just in time." Charlotte exhaled, then exhaled again, trying to expel her rage. "Otherwise, I might have been arrested for assault."

"I think you've had enough excitement for one day," Lydia said in her quiet, level voice.

"Probably." Grace let loose a weird little giggle that said she'd been pushed way beyond her limit.

"Your hands are cold." Spencer rubbed them gently, as if Grace suffered from August frostbite. "I'll walk you to your car."

Suddenly, Charlotte's last scrap of strength fluttered away. She longed to sit on the sidewalk too, but she feared she'd never get up.

"Here, lean on me," Lydia said. She was thin but stronger than Charlotte had thought. She supported Charlotte while Spencer helped Grace to her feet and took her arm in his.

They all walked down the street as if they'd aged twenty years.

"We'd better hurry," Charlotte said suddenly. "We need to get home before Winnie finds out."

"Where are my girls?" Winnie called from the foyer of the inn.

Charlotte raised her groggy head from a sofa pillow and groaned. "I'm in the living room." She shifted her feet to the carpeted floor.

Winnie swooped into the room, basket in one hand. Tears rolled down her cheeks, and her eyes blazed like those of an avenging angel. Dropping the basket, her aunt hauled Charlotte to her feet and gave her a rib-cracking embrace.

Despite the lack of oxygen, Charlotte melted into Winnie's hug.

Grace, also appearing groggy, walked into the room a minute later to receive the same lung-crushing love.

While Charlotte basked in her aunt's joy, a tiny stopwatch in the corner of her mind counted down the seconds until the inevitable explosion.

Winnie beat the clock. "I can't believe Tom and Bonnie would do such horrible things. They stayed under your roof and ate your food. Yet they stole from you and lied. Pulled a gun on you. Threatened to throw you into the ocean—"

A gentle tap on the living room door interrupted Winnie's angry rant. Spencer.

Charlotte, whose head hadn't yet cleared, had forgotten he'd manned the phone so they could catch a nap. Though a grin tugged at the corners of Spencer's mouth, his eyes looked a little worried.

When Winnie went to the foyer, searching for a tissue to dry her tears, Grace whispered, "It's okay, Spencer."

The nervousness left his face.

Charlotte didn't doubt that he'd tried to talk Winnie into waiting a while before coming inside, but he may as well have tried to stop a freight train.

Although this freight train had come bearing a basket that surely contained some of Winnie's best goodies.

When her aunt returned, Charlotte encircled her with an arm. "All that excitement made me hungry."

"Have you eaten anything since breakfast? Well, we'll just have to do something about that." Winnie picked up her basket and marched off to the kitchen.

"I'll help you in a minute," Spencer called, then faced Charlotte and Grace. "We'll get your plates ready while you both talk to Captain Daley."

"Thank you." Grace had said very little, but Charlotte heard a world of gratitude in those two words.

Spencer smiled. "You're very welcome."

After Spencer headed for the kitchen, Charlotte said, "Are you sure you're up to this?"

"Of course." A shade of Grace's usual efficiency returned. "We'll call the captain and put him on speakerphone."

The first thing Captain Daley said amounted to a major apology. "I'm so sorry. I never should have let you ladies accost the Kleins."

"It's not your fault. You didn't make us go downtown," Grace reminded him. "But how did you know we were in danger?"

"You sounded strange when I talked to you on the phone," Daley said.

Charlotte was so thankful that Grace had been able to clue Daley in on what was going on and where they were before Bonnie made her hang up. "How did Spencer get there so fast?"

"I called him immediately," the captain said. "He happened to be downtown, so he arrived at almost the same time as my officers and I did."

Charlotte nodded. So that was why their neighbor had shown up in such a timely fashion.

"Spencer would have checked on you anyway," Daley continued. "So I thought I might as well give him permission."

Grace's cheeks colored a little. "Well, he certainly appeared at the right moment."

"Yes, he did," the captain said. "I'm sorry I didn't warn you about the Kleins. You shouldn't have been in that dangerous situation."

"Spencer said the thefts hadn't involved any firearms," Grace said. "You had no reason to suspect Bonnie would threaten us with a gun."

Neither did we. Charlotte still scratched her head over the pleasant thief turned violent.

"True, but that was before we took their fingerprints." His phone crackled as he exhaled. "Between Spencer and me, we found out the Kleins might have been busy for a long, long time—far more than a decade. Spencer just finished tracking down a 1970s connection between them and some small paintings stolen by the Nazis during World War II. Not entirely sure yet how deeply these two were involved in the resale. But a go-between ended up dead."

Charlotte choked, and Grace paled.

"Got a couple of other instances where it appears the Kleins pulled off minor art heists," Daley went on. "The thefts occurred years apart, so they probably took place on European research trips while they were professors. More on that as we talk with Interpol."

Charlotte closed her eyes. The international police organization was after Tom and Bonnie? But they'd never even mentioned going to Europe. They'd talked only about South America.

"The big thing that's surfaced is a Swiss bank account with 3 million dollars in it." The captain paused. "Their fingerprints access it."

Charlotte gaped.

"So that's why Bonnie was willing to do anything to protect their business," Grace commented. "She said she'd always lived life her way and wasn't going to change now."

"You got it," Daley said. "As we dig more, we'll probably find evidence of who knows how many other jobs they've pulled. Though I imagine they toned it down some as they got older."

"Especially since Tom was losing the ability to hold up his end," Grace said. "I wonder if Bonnie has always controlled him."

Charlotte didn't feel much sympathy for the old man. "Tom had a choice when he was younger. He made the wrong one."

"What about the driver of the van?" Grace asked. "Who is he?"

"Bob Claremont is Bonnie's brother," the captain answered. "He owns a company near Philadelphia. He concealed the loot in his warehouse for a share of the profits. Sometimes he hid the stolen goods for years while the Kleins waited for investigations to grow cold. Then they'd sell them."

"What an operation," Charlotte said.

"I believe the police in Philadelphia will find your sampler soon," Daley said. "Bob is cooperating in hopes of reducing his prison sentence."

"That's wonderful news," Grace said. "Thank you."

"But be warned that we won't be able to release it to you until the trials are finished," the captain added.

"We understand," Charlotte said.

They talked about the confidentiality of the information Daley had shared. "When we've lined up a little more evidence, I'll hold a press conference. You can attend if you want. I'll brief you on what cannot be made public. But please keep all of this quiet until then. And until you testify in court."

Charlotte still couldn't quite grasp the fact that they were talking about prosecuting Tom and Bonnie. She knew her sister found it even harder to believe.

"Only a few days ago, Bonnie helped me fold towels," Grace said. "Just this morning, Tom was sitting at our table, gobbling up Charlotte's blueberry scones."

"As a cop, you think you've seen everything." A note of shock still colored the captain's voice. "Guess I hadn't. Hope I won't see anything like this again for a long, long time."

"Charlotte Wylde, what in the world have you and your sister been up to?" Dean, bursting through their back door without a knock, sounded like a big brother. He entered the kitchen and crossed his arms.

Charlotte, hastily arranging hors d'oeuvres on a baking sheet, stopped and sighed. "Did Captain Daley call you?"

"Yeah, he told me about the Kleins." He whistled. "Who would have thought?"

"Not us," Charlotte said as she set the oven timer. "Until all the red flags in their background started popping up."

Dean walked over to her and gently grasped her by the shoulders. "What were you and Grace thinking, going after criminals like that?"

She couldn't help but like the worry in his probing eyes as well as the scent of his woodsy aftershave. Nevertheless, she backed away. "We weren't going after them. We were only trying to keep them from skipping town. You know, until the captain could find enough evidence against them."

"Well, the next time you decide to play detective, take me along," Dean said.

"I hope there won't be a next time," Charlotte said. "Has the captain found any trace of your clock?"

"Not yet," he replied. "I guess the Kleins have stolen more than small antiques, so he's got bigger stuff to tackle right now. But he promised to look into it soon."

Charlotte cautioned herself to say little, since she didn't know how much the captain had told him. "I hope we get the sampler back."

"Daley's a good man. He'll do whatever he can to recover our things." Dean shook his head. "I still can't believe this. Now every time somebody registers and asks for a senior discount, I'll have to check them out with the FBI."

Not to mention Interpol. She didn't mention that either.

Winnie called out from the back door. Her aunt had fed them sandwiches, but after deciding their survival called for a celebration—whether they wanted one or not—she had gone home to get a few more things.

Charlotte and Dean rushed to the door. Winnie's arms were full, so they relieved her of her load.

Grace and Spencer, whom she'd pressed into positioning tables and chairs and decorating the veranda, came in for an iced tea break.

Having assembled a sufficient audience, Winnie produced a giant plastic cake keeper. "Look what I brought." With the air of a magician, she lifted the top, revealing a quadruple-layer coconut cake.

Though Charlotte had tasted—and made—gourmet desserts for years, her mouth watered, and she itched to sample the snowy frosting.

"The best cake in the world," Winnie told Dean. "My mama's recipe. The only cake fit for this party. I knew last night that I made it for something special." She hugged and kissed her nieces.

As Winnie removed piles of food from her bags, Grace said, "Goodness, what will we do with all this if no one comes?"

"I called Mimi and Patty and told them we'd start about six." Winnie grinned. "Word will get around."

Charlotte exchanged looks with Grace. Telling Mimi and Patty about the party meant the whole town would show up and possibly the populations of neighboring counties.

Charlotte elbowed her sister. "At least we're not serving sturgeon caviar."

They chuckled.

Another knock sounded at the back door.

Charlotte answered it.

A sheepish Ian twirled his beret. The patio chair behind him was loaded with bags of groceries. "I am so sorry to be late in returning. I encountered one of my historical colleagues downtown and lost track of time. Did I miss the poker tournament?"

23

Grace

Grace had hoped against hope that after such a late night—the last party attendees hadn't left until after midnight—Ian, like the other guests, would sleep in the next morning. But deep inside her innkeeper's bones, Grace knew better.

Sure enough, Ian appeared in the dining room bright and early. "Good morning," she said.

He answered her with an intense look that awakened her more than the caffeine. "A good morning to you, dear lady. I cannot tell you how thankful I am to see you safe and in good health."

At the party, the story of yesterday's calamities had stunned Ian into an extended silence. After surprising Grace with a fierce embrace, he'd left for the rest of the evening. With an inward chuckle, she recalled that Spencer didn't seem to mind his absence.

Now, though, as she felt Ian's gaze on her, she almost wished Tom and Bonnie would bustle in.

Almost.

"Would you like breakfast?" Grace asked, changing the subject. Charlotte had declared that she wouldn't rise early to cook for Ian alone, but she'd baked a crabmeat casserole last night before she went home.

"That would be wonderful," he answered.

Grace heated up a generous piece of casserole and poured a cup of the strong coffee she'd brewed for herself, then handed the plate and cup to Ian. "Maybe you'd like to eat on the veranda? It's still cool and such a beautiful morning."

He cocked his head. "One of your favorite spots?"

"Oh yes," Grace answered before she thought.

"Then perhaps you could join me for a few minutes." Before Ian had drawn her with boyish appeal. Now his eyes issued a man's invitation.

Both worked, she had to admit. Grace poured herself a cup of coffee.

Winston trailed after them as they sought chairs where they could watch the sunlight dancing on the lake.

Though Winston clearly liked Ian, he settled down at Grace's feet, soothing her disquiet.

On one hand, she was grateful for the silence. On the other, she wished Ian would say his piece and get it over with.

A few minutes later, he asked, "Have you heard any news about the recovery of your sampler?"

An odd disappointment quieted her throbbing pulse. "Captain Daley believes they will find it soon."

Ian brightened. "So he knows where the sampler is? And maybe the clock?"

Typical Ian—concerned with the all-important rescue of antiques. "Yes, it sounds like he does."

"Their scheme was clever." Ian scowled. "And diabolical."

"At least they won't steal anymore." That thought made her feel good all over. "And though the police won't release our sampler until the trials are finished, Charlotte and I should get it back."

He fell silent again, and Grace wondered if he'd noticed she hadn't displayed the sampler he'd given her. He must have. How awkward.

Amid her internal debate about whether to hang it, Ian said, "When your sampler is released, would you consider selling it to me for $50,000?"

She stared. That amount would shore up their reserve fund considerably, but . . . "No, I believe I told you it's not for sale. Not at any price."

Ian didn't act surprised. "Would you mind telling me why?"

Grace explained that it was her mother's favorite verse. She told him how her mother had refereed the quarrels she and Charlotte had fought as children by reminding them of the words.

Ian grinned, something he didn't often do.

That boyish charm again. *Stop it.*

As if at her command, his smile waned. "Spats aside, you and your sister seem quite devoted to each other. I was an only child, so I missed out."

Grace recalled Charlotte's caviar crusade. "I'll be glad to let you sub for me during our next disagreement."

"Really?"

Grace blinked. Was he joking?

"I beg your pardon," Ian said. "I only meant that I envy the closeness, even if you quarrel sometimes." He hesitated. "I owe my late mother a great deal. She encouraged me in my studies. Still, we shared a distant relationship, almost as distant as with my absent father."

"I'm so sorry to hear that," Grace said.

"I had never witnessed such closeness before I came here. Perhaps that is why I have been drawn to you." He leaned toward her. "You connect with everyone. You see into their very souls, then do what you can to help them." His voice, though softer, intensified. "You saw into mine."

Charlotte had told Grace to think about it before saying yes if Ian asked her out on a date. Grace had rolled her eyes at her sister's crazy directive. But was it so crazy after all?

This man was in earnest. Vulnerable as a child.

God, please help me.

"Rather than my seeing into your soul, maybe you are seeing inside yourself," she suggested gently. "You're realizing that you want to know and be known."

The light in his face dimmed. "Perhaps that is true. For me, history was always enough. Teaching was enough. But now, I think there could be more."

"Maybe it's your time to explore and learn about closeness." Grace paused, then said, "I don't think this is the time you should commit to a long-distance relationship. Do you?" *It's certainly not my time. And please don't shorten the distance. Stay in Illinois.*

Ian slumped in his chair and sighed. "No. I suppose not. I shall leave as soon as I pack my things."

Grace bit her lip, wishing she could say something to cheer him. She hadn't realized Winston had risen from his spot to nose Ian's knee.

At first, the historian absently scratched the dog's ear, but when he whined, Ian glanced into his face. "So, Winston, you have your mistress's intelligence. A kind heart like hers as well."

Grace brightened. A nice tribute to Winston. "Thank you. Winston is truly a remarkable dog."

"But she is kind enough not to raise false hopes," Ian continued. "Though I do hope we might remain friends."

"I would like that," Grace said.

Charlotte poked her head out the door and froze.

Grace ignored the panic on her sister's face. "Ian and I have been enjoying the view and talking. What a shame he'll be leaving us later today."

"A shame. Oh yes." Charlotte hurried to the historian, who stood. To Grace's surprise, her sister extended her hand to him. "I wanted to apologize before you left. Despite the lack of evidence, I assumed you were guilty. That was inexcusable, and I'm very sorry."

Gallant as always, Ian bowed over her hand. "We all err from time to time. I am happy to continue this house's tradition of forgiveness."

After he made his exit, Charlotte whispered, "What was he talking about? And what did he say to you?"

Relieved and tired beyond measure, Grace waved her off. "I'll explain later. Right now, I'm going to pour myself another cup of coffee, sit for a few minutes, and relearn how to breathe."

Until Ian actually drove out of sight, Grace feared he would stay—especially when, upon seeking her and Charlotte for a final goodbye, he found them hanging his sampler in the hallway.

He smiled. "I am indeed honored."

The historian, however, had obviously understood that Grace would not change her mind. With a promise to stay in touch, a bow, and a brief kiss on the back of Grace's hand, he left for home.

Charlotte went back to her cottage.

Grace barely had time to debate her feelings over Ian's departure when a familiar car drove up.

She stood at a window as Daniel and Maggie exited the car and slowly approached the inn's front entrance.

She didn't give them time to open the door. Instead, she dashed over and threw it open. "Daniel! Maggie!" She hugged them like long-lost relatives. "I'm so glad to see you again."

Maggie clung to Grace. "I'm really sorry we left the way we did."

"It wasn't her fault," Daniel said. "It was my idea. I thought it would be better if we went to stay with my relatives in Atlanta for a little while."

"You were just trying to protect me." Maggie turned to Grace.

The young woman's cheeks were flushed. "Did the police captain tell you about—"

"The mistakes you made as a teen?" Grace interrupted. "Yes, and I'm sure you're not the first to make them. You don't need to worry about any accusations from us or from the police."

"Thank you," Maggie said. "I can't tell you how much we appreciate it."

"Did you hear about the Kleins?" Grace asked, changing the sensitive subject.

"No," Daniel said. "What about them?"

Grace summarized the unbelievable events that had recently taken place.

For a moment, the two seemed to forget their own angst. Daniel emitted a long whistle, and Maggie appeared shocked.

"Who would have suspected Tom and Bonnie? They were so sweet." Maggie shuddered. "I don't think I want to hear all the awful details."

"Good. I'd rather not review them." Grace touched the young woman's arm. "Would you like something cold to drink?"

Maggie nodded.

Grace led the couple into the coolness of the living room, then went to the kitchen and poured three glasses of lemonade.

When she returned, Daniel and Maggie were sitting on the sofa. Grace gave them their drinks and took a seat in a chair. "I'm so sorry your stay here didn't turn out as well as you'd hoped," she said, breaking what threatened to become an awkward silence.

"Oh, we had a wonderful time here," Maggie said, then frowned. "Until Papa came."

Daniel gently rubbed his wife's shoulder. "Until then, we hadn't really considered the police might suspect Maggie had stolen the sampler or the clock. I suppose her father thought he was protecting her too." He gave a wry smile. "Neither of us did a great job of it."

"It's not your fault I took those things," Maggie reminded him. "Even if Papa was a control freak, I should have chosen a different way."

"You did in college, remember?" Daniel said. "Don't beat yourself up about it."

"At any rate," Grace said, "you still have a room here for the weekend, if you want it."

"We can stay?" Maggie asked.

Grace hugged the couple. "Of course. We've missed you."

"Thank you," Maggie said, dabbing her eyes.

"What are we waiting for?" Daniel said. "Let's get our bags." He led Maggie to the car.

A few minutes later, Grace watched as they joyously walked back inside with their luggage and hauled it upstairs.

Hopefully, Daniel and Maggie would end their honeymoon on a positive note. They certainly needed it.

Thinking about the challenges they faced in dealing with Maggie's father reminded Grace how tired she was.

Still, little rest materialized for the weary. After Grace called Charlotte and told her their guests had returned, they were summoned to the police station, where Captain Daley recorded formal interviews. Back at the inn, they answered phone calls from the prosecutor's office and increasing requests from reporters.

"I'm so glad there's no social hour tonight," Grace remarked as she leaned against the kitchen counter. Lydia had gone out for the day and wasn't expected back until later this evening, and Daniel and Maggie were celebrating Maggie's vindication at Turner's Lakeside Grill.

"Me too," Charlotte said.

Grace pulled her phone from her pocket and set it on the counter. "As of now, this thing is off for the rest of the evening."

"Good idea. Now what can we have for supper?" Charlotte peered into the refrigerator. "There's crabmeat left over from this morning's casserole. Why don't I throw together a couple of sandwiches?"

"Sounds great." Grace was well aware that anything Charlotte whipped up would rival a top restaurant's best offerings.

Grace poured two tall glasses of sweet tea while Charlotte made the sandwiches. Winston followed them out to the veranda, where they sat eating and gazing at the lake.

"Okay, I let you finish every last bite." Charlotte eyed Grace. "Now tell me everything Ian said."

Grace laughed. "I suppose I have to earn my crabmeat sandwich." Censoring their conversation only a little, she repeated it. "I hadn't thought of the inn as a 'house of forgiveness,' but looking back on our guests—and our own lives—it's obvious."

"Me either," Charlotte said, smiling. "But it's a nice idea."

Grace shifted in her chair. She was afraid her sister wouldn't like what she had to say next. "Mom was right, you know. The Bible says we should always forgive. That's why I'm going to visit Tom and Bonnie."

Charlotte gaped at her. "What? Why would you go see them after everything they've done?" She proceeded to rant about Tom and Bonnie and all the trouble they had caused.

Grace listened, reasoned, and soothed until Charlotte finally calmed somewhat.

"If you're fool enough to visit them in jail, then I'm going with you," Charlotte declared as she wiped her eyes.

Grace hadn't expected that. Maybe Charlotte was taking the first step on the path of forgiveness too.

"If I don't go, those liars will con you into paying for their lawyer," Charlotte added.

Grace smiled. Well, maybe it was a baby step on the path of forgiveness. She got up and gave her sister a hug. "Thank you."

"There you two are." Winnie appeared with a big tote and a pitcher of tea. She replenished their glasses and sat down beside them, drinking her own unsweetened version. "That was quite a party last night."

They discussed the get-together, and Grace told Winnie about Ian's departure and Daniel and Maggie's arrival. Then they talked about Tom and Bonnie.

"I'm proud of you girls for deciding to go and see them," Winnie said. "Your mother would be proud too."

They grew quiet for a while, lost in their own thoughts. After a tempestuous day that had only grown stormier, the silence seemed a blessed change.

Lydia walked onto the veranda, interrupting their reverie. "I'm sorry. I didn't mean to intrude."

"Not at all. Please join us." Grace smiled. "Would you like a glass of tea?"

"No thank you," Lydia answered as she took a seat next to Winnie.

"Did you have a nice day?" Charlotte asked.

Lydia nodded. "I went driving to clear my head. It's so beautiful here."

"It certainly is," Winnie said.

Lydia gave Winnie a small smile and took her hand in hers. "I meant to thank you for trying to give me that baby quilt."

"Have you decided whether you want it?" Winnie asked.

"I'd love it," Lydia replied. "That is, if you still want to give it."

"Of course." Winnie pulled the quilt from her tote and handed it to Lydia.

Grace and Charlotte exchanged knowing glances. How very like Winnie to carry the quilt around, waiting for the opportune time to bestow it on its intended recipient.

Smiling, Lydia stroked its softness with her fingertips. "I suppose this won't make sense until I explain the difficult season I've been experiencing," she said, her smile fading.

"We have been concerned about you," Grace ventured.

"Though I didn't show it much, I appreciated your kindness," Lydia said. "But I'm afraid that I had mostly myself to blame."

Winnie patted the woman's shoulder. "You don't have to talk about it. We respect your privacy."

"I want to get it off my chest." Lydia took a deep breath. "Ellie, my only child, did quite well at Yale during her first two years. But she suddenly quit school and married a man she'd just met."

In Lydia's eyes, that probably seemed the worst thing her daughter could have done. No wonder she had struggled with Daniel and Maggie's newlywed bliss.

"Ellie didn't invite me to her wedding last winter. She knew I would have refused to attend." Lydia wrung her hands. "I haven't heard from her since. After the things I said, I don't know if Ellie will ever speak to me again."

A vivid picture of a furious Lydia rose in Grace's mind—Lydia and the brawny young man. "Did you meet with her husband while you were here?"

"Yes, I talked to Cody." Lydia tilted her head. "How did you know?"

"I'm sorry, but I overheard a little of your argument with him while I was walking with Winston," Grace explained. "Did he come all this way to see you?"

"He did. Cody travels often for his job, and he happened to be in Charleston for a few days so he drove here." A single tear trickled down Lydia's cheek. "He told me they're expecting a baby. I'd already found out from my cousin. Ellie's close to her daughter."

Grace put a hand over her heart. A baby. Lydia's first grandchild, a child she might never know.

"But somehow his showing up made me even angrier. I assumed he'd come to beg for money. I know they'll have more expenses when the baby arrives." Lydia bowed her head and sobbed. "Now I realize Cody was trying to bridge the Grand Canyon between us."

As Charlotte gave Lydia a handful of tissues, Winston sat down in front of their guest and whined softly.

"Aren't you sweet?" Still crying, Lydia reached down and petted the dog.

Winston wagged his tail, then curled up at Lydia's feet.

"Do you remember when I told you that I visited the hospital here?" Lydia asked Grace between sobs.

Fighting her own tears, Grace nodded.

"I went to the nursery and saw four little babies. They were so tiny and beautiful," Lydia continued. "Their grandparents came to see them and hold them. But I may never hold mine." She flooded the little quilt with her tears.

Finally, Winnie placed a hand on her arm. "You must call Ellie and Cody."

"It won't do any good," Lydia protested. "They'll hang up."

"Then call them again. And again." Winnie took her by the shoulders and stared her straight in the eye. "Never stop calling. You can't give up and let your family fall apart."

Eventually, the tears narrowed to delicate rivulets. Lydia sighed. "You're right. I'd better try now, or I'll talk myself out of it."

"It'll be okay," Winnie said. "You'll see."

Lydia pulled her phone from her purse. "I hope Ellie hasn't changed her number or blocked me. Not that I'd blame her." She rose and tapped the phone, then hurried around the corner of the veranda.

Grace closed her eyes and felt prayers wafting around her.

The silence seemed to last a year.

"Ellie?"

Grace cringed at the pain and longing in that one word.

"Oh, Ellie, I am so sorry," Lydia choked out. "Can you ever forgive me?"

Grace opened her eyes. Lydia must have walked away because her voice faded into the distance.

Charlotte turned to her sister and aunt. "Want some more tea?" Without waiting for an answer, she refilled their glasses.

Winnie leaned back and pointed out stars that were trying to outdo each other's twinkles.

When Lydia returned, she was beaming. "I'm going to see my daughter and son-in-law next week."

"That's wonderful news!" Winnie exclaimed. She jumped up and embraced Lydia.

The women chatted excitedly about Lydia's reunion with her family and her future grandchild.

Grace was overjoyed that the Magnolia Harbor Inn had worked its magic in the lives of their guests once again. "There's nothing like sharing sweet tea with family and friends on a summer night." She smiled and took a sip. "And I think this might be the sweetest I've ever tasted."